MY Summer ROMANCE

ANUSHKA AGRAWAL

Published By :
Aksharansh Publication
An imprint of kharidobecho.in
Hinjewadi Phase - 3, Pune (M.H.) - 411057
Tel : (020) - 41243975, Mo : +91-7380434014

ISBN : **978-93-92445-86-6**

Processed & printed in India

ACKNOWLEDGEMENT

I would like to express my special thanks and gratitude towards my father who has paid for everything despite the harsh struggles financially. I would like to thank my mother who supported my passion and fought for it like it was hers and my younger brother who did everything to make me laugh when I felt low. They had been a constant support. They trusted me and encouraged me through every phase of my life.

I would like to thank my best friend Samyak for being the most amazing gift that god has ever granted me. I would like to thank Talha and Shantidoot who were my saviours and only reasons I stayed alive while being bullied and harassed. Without you all my dreams would have never turned into reality.

I would love to thank all my readers for choosing this book.

The beauty in my life
Comes from all of you
You bring thoughts into my mind
That last for a lifetime.
Thank you for being a part of my life.

Contents

CHAPTER 1

FEELS

ROSHNI… her name meant the sunshine but the days of her life were an irony to what her name meant.

It had been raining heavily that night. She stood there on the pavement admiring the rain. She did not like the rain when she was a child and the rainy season used to be her enemy because humidity and mud annoyed her. As the years passed, there she was admiring the rain she never thought she would. There was a time when her heart was innocent and she knew nothing about love, there was a time where she had an option to like and dislike things, but as we all know time changes people and new things take form while the old things fade away.

The only thought that took over her mind at that particular moment was leaving umbrella and getting wet in the rain. Before anyone could imagine she was out there doing what she wanted to, doing what made her happy. She folded her umbrella and kept it aside. The street was empty and dark with few artificial lights providing a dim view of the world around. It had been a few years now that she had developed this love for nature. She stepped out in the rain and opened her arms wide and looked up at the sky. Rain drops trickled down her face and the coolness of it made her forget everything for a while and she relaxed. After a long time, a smile emerged on her lips. And she felt the rain like no one else did.

It hadn't been long and soon the realization struck upon her that it was late and her mom was waiting for her at home. She rushed towards her umbrella and walked home briskly. The street was glowing because of the rain but she had no time to endure it. The door of her house was open and she quickly tip toed inside her room and slipped herself into a comfortable night gown. Her mom was so busy in the kitchen that she had no clue that Roshni was home. Seeing her mom work so much she hugged her mom from behind. "How much will you work mum? Is the dinner still not ready? Would you like me to help you out?" Her mom turned around and gave her a genial smile and directed her to do some work. Roshni was the only child of her parents. Her dad was a civil engineer and had been out of station since a week now for some business purpose. It had been 5 years that they shifted to Kerala.

After dinner she sat on a chair in the balcony feeling the wind around her and looking at the beautiful full moon. She whispered in the ears of heaven a secret known by none. When she looked at the moon her eyes felt relieved because she believed that the person looking at the moon at the same time as she did was the person who could read her eyes. She was a writer but her eyes said it all and if not her eyes, her smile was enough to read her heart. She whispered in the ears of heaven to help him reach her, the one she was destined to be with. The one who just comes and holds her hand and tells her that 'everything will be alright'. The only one who ever told this to her was she herself in front of the mirror when her face dripped with tears and no one could see her. Her love was unconditional and beautiful. She didn't regret giving it to anyone she met because she knew everyone had a heart and all of them needed love and care. Once her friend asked her, "you write so well and it can make a person feel so special, I wonder what a guy will have to do to impress you". She didn't speak anything, just gave a smile which was enough to give that answer to her soul. Little did they know that a person like her who only gave and never expected or got anything in return can be made the happiest person on earth by just a small gesture. Little did they know that she enjoyed and loved everything to show the people how beautiful the world around them was, and little did they know that she enjoyed every moment because she had lost many before and she was afraid to lose those beautiful moments again. Little things hurt her but as the world said she believed that it made her strong. She cried to let her feelings out and put her eyes at ease but she never met anyone who could actually understand that. Maybe she cried too much, maybe she smiled too much, maybe she loved too much, maybe she dreamed too much. Maybe that's what was hurting her but it wasn't what she chose for herself.

"Roshni, go and sleep baby it is too late you have college tomorrow", her thoughts were interrupted by her mom's call and she pushed all of those aside. With just hope in her heart she went to sleep.

The sky had been clear and as she walked into the class. Natasha held her wrist and pulled her to one of the back benches where Meghna was waiting for them. Meghna and Natasha were Roshni's best friends since high school and the only two people in college who she trusted. It was in class 9 that they met and became friends in one of the school trips to the beach. They ended up taking the same stream to pursue their career in commerce in Omega University. Before Roshni could even sit, they started talking, "OMG! Did you see the new guy, Druv who joined college, he is so cute." Roshni looked at them completely clueless. "Roshni, don't tell me that you didn't see him. How could you not notice him?" As soon as those words left Meghna's mouth, Natasha kicked Roshni's leg and made her look in the opposite direction where she saw the new guy. After a glance, she turned to them, "what is so special about him? He is cute but who knows what kind of a heart he has and it is better you guys don't get your hearts broken by that fellow", she said pointing towards his direction. The conversation didn't seem important to her so she just went and took her seat in one of the front benches. Meghna and Natasha got pissed a little probably but they would be fine she knew. The day was boring as usual with hours of lectures and a short recess.

A week later she met Manasvi. They often went for a walk together and she lived near her house. Although they met each other rarely they shared everything with each other. Manasvi had completed her 12th and was doing BCom in JC college, "Druv you say haan? Wait a minute, I have heard that name before. What is his last name?" "Mehta", she replied. "Omg! He joined your college? He was in my college. I know that guy real well. He was in our college for 4 years and is from Dubai. The girls of our college fell for him because he is cute." "That's what is happening here too and guess what even Natasha and Meghna find him cute." "Is it? Tell them to be careful because trust me, he is not someone who can be trusted. He had like two to three girlfriends in college and he broke each of their hearts." "What?" Roshni was shocked.

She knew guys like him can only play with the emotions of girls and those were the last kind of people who she could bear.

Druv was one of the back benchers and knowing about him from Manasvi made Roshni avoid talking to him. He tried talking to her once or twice but she gave him short replies to just end the conversation which eventually made even Druv hesitant to talk to her. The only thing that bothered Roshni was his eyes. They were mesmerizing and enough to draw any girl close to him. But all she did was deny that fact too because she knew that Manasvi can never lie to her.

***

"Guys listen I got a news. Druv and Nandini got committed", said Meghna. On hearing that, the only thing that was on Roshni's mind was that it had not even been a month that Druv joined college and he got a girlfriend for himself. She never believed that love can happen in first site she was an old college romantic. She used to always wonder if love at first site was ever anything more than being interested in someone's body. However, the girl didn't know that so wished that Nandini does not get hurt. Nandini was the most beautiful girl of their class and her beauty could catch any guy's attention and so it did catch Druv's. Roshni trusted Manasvi more than anyone and believed that Druv was faking it all. But sometimes seeing them together for once even Roshni thought that maybe Druv had true feelings for Nandini.

"What? OMG when did they even start talking? I had no idea they got so close" said Natasha.

"Guys, Druv is not a good guy you can never trust him. The other day I met Manasvi and she told me that he was in her college and had cheated on all the girls he got committed with."

"What? Really? OMG thank god I didn't fall for him. He was always so sweet to me", Meghna said.

"But the thing is maybe this time he is serious about Nandini because she is one of the best he can have and seeing them together all the time doesn't seem like he is faking it" Roshni said. Wondering if the thoughts were because of the reality or because she wanted to believe in his genuineness for his obvious glances and oh so good looks.

"Chuck that! How about we all go for a picnic this weekend. Classes have become way too boring and we need a break from our daily routines, only the three of us what say?", asked Natasha. "Yeah", she replied.

Natasha's dad owned a farmhouse situated in the outskirts of Kerela which was their destination for the weekend.

***

"Roshni, hurry up we are waiting", came Natasha's voice.

Roshni took her bag and rushed downstairs, "bye mom, I will be back soon". Three of them sat in the cab and took off. By the time they reached, it was sunset and they sat on the wooden benches in the porch sipping coffee and talking.

"It's been so long that I have felt this relaxed" Roshni said. Her favourite times of the vacations were the sipping of coffee that made everything feel so still. After a while when her friends went back to rest, she looked around the twinkling stars and wondered if the Night had some magical healing powers to take away all the stress from her.

***

The next day Roshni was the first one to wake up. "Guys wake up! Look at the weather it is so good let's go for boating today", she pulled away Natasha and Meghna's blankets and pushed them to freshen up.

The sky was clear and the water in the lake was shining with the reflection of the sun. Quickly they leased a boat and drifted away. The lake twisted in an S shape with huge trees on either side which made the scene appear magical. Roshni's heart smiled thinking it must be the most peaceful place on earth. Natasha put her hand inside the water and sprinkled it on Meghna. Retaliating, Meghna stood up which made the boat shake and Roshni intentionally pushed Meghna out into the water. Roshni and Natasha burst out laughing seeing Meghna pissed and soon the three girls were swimming in the lake laughing and teasing each other. They had brunch in Sunrise café and finally booked a cab and headed home.

"This was the best weekend that I had till now it was so peaceful away from the crowd and hustle", said Roshni while her mom was watching TV. Her mom made Roshni put her head on her lap and caressed her hair, "always stay happy like this my sweetheart".

CHAPTER 2

MET THE EYE

She felt his eyes on her. She knew he was watching. She felt her heart flutter and a chill rushed down her spine making her shiver. She didn't look back. She knew that if she turned around she would give herself to him. She was scared of being hurt. All her past experiences raced in her mind of how she was always left alone. Fortunately, her past was strong enough to stop her from looking back.

A week had passed and Druv was made to sit in the bench right behind Roshni and the only thing he did was stare, which made Roshni really uncomfortable and conscious. The bell rang and it was recess.

"Lee Min Ho Oppa is the best he is so cute. Did you watch City Hunter?" said Meghna

"I like Woo Bin Oppa more and the best series is Healer. Trust me girl you won't find anything better than that" Roshni said.

One reason why Roshni and Meghna became good friends was because of their interest in Korean dramas. They rarely met people who loved Korean series while Roshni liked English TV shows like Friends and Arrow too. She always appreciated the versatility in her life. The three of them pulled chairs and took their seats in the canteen. Roshni was having her lunch but then suddenly she saw Druv, who was walking towards her.

"Roshni, Can you please give me your Economics notes? You see I joined college a little late so I don't really have them and everyone told me you can help", said Druv

"Yeah sure I will get a copy for you tomorrow", Roshni was surprised at how easily his charms made him blurt those words out.

"Cool" he said and Nandini came swooping into his arms out of nowhere, taking away his attention. In a minute, they drifted off.

***

After reaching home Roshni was surfing on the internet when a notification beeped. It was a friend request from Druv. Facing Druv every single day in college was turning out to be tough for her because it eventually attracted her towards him. An eye contact for a girl means a lot more than it does to a guy she knew it and the fact that Druv stared at her even when she wasn't looking made her think about him even more. Druv had already started taking control over her mind and she didn't know what she should do to control her feelings. Giving him short replies even didn't help anymore. She sighed and accepted the friend request. He obviously couldn't hold him responsible for staring and deny the request.

Since Roshni was 11 years old, she had been left alone and betrayed by all the people she trusted, most of them came to be her best friends. People didn't trust her and give her the love she deserved which is why she had turned out to be sensitive girl and cared too much that her words shouldn't hurt any person around her. Her mom and Dad were with her when she went through the dark days of her life but she really could not tell them as she knew it would hurt them more to see their daughter suffering. The only thing she wanted to do and focus on was her studies and career so that one day her parents are proud of having her as their daughter. The harsh struggles of a middle class family were very well understood by her parents and she wanted to earn them a good standard of living. Falling for Druv was the last thing she ever wanted to do because getting hurt was obvious for her and she could not risk her studies.

"Roshni, let's go out and have ice cream today", her mom called out.

"Yes, mumma." She sighed. The usual excitement didn't touch her probably because she was never a big fan of ice cream but maybe chocolate did the work for her.

The ice cream parlour was more crowded than usual.

"One butterscotch and one chocolate please", Roshni ordered.

"Roshni you shouldn't eat so much chocolates."

"Mom this one last time", Roshni pleaded and her cuteness made her mom smile and kiss her forehead.

***

"Roshni, I owe you a treat for those notes."

"No no it is alright you don't have to…" She said scanning the canteen to see if she noticed any classmates.

"Oh c'mon", Druv insisted. "Fine" she said.

The canteen was in its usual bustle. Roshni and Druv made their way to the cake counter. It was amusing how both preferred the same flavoured cakes and drinks. Both of them talked about their colleges and Druv was good at making Roshni laugh. It made Roshni happy talking to him. He treated her like a lady and was a complete gentleman to her. He heard and understood everything she talked about much better than others could.

"Druv! All this time you had been in the canteen and I was looking for you", Nandini's voice came from behind Roshni.

" I am so sorry sweetheart…", Druv apologized.

Roshni got up from her seat and excused herself as she didn't want to intrude.

"I am sorry Roshni." Druv said.

"It is totally okay I can understand" she smiled worried if she made a wrong impression on Nandini for eating with her boyfriend.

***

"Roshni! What's wrong? You seem so lost today", Natasha said.

"Nothing. I just want some time alone with myself" she said

Meghna and Natasha knew that something was really wrong but Roshni wasn't telling anything because the two things Roshni hated were being alone and being in the dark.

"Ok fine let us know if you need something" they went back to their benches.

Seeing Nandini and Druv together sometimes bothered Roshni and she could do nothing but stay silent. She denied the fact that she started liking Druv because accepting that fact will only hurt her. One because Druv loved Nandini and second because Druv was not the kind of person who took relationships seriously.

1 month later

She started liking to spend time with him and when he asked for some help with concepts she didn't want to deny it. Not like he would suddenly care about her more than being a nerd. She didn't feel like she needed to draw lines any longer because she felt tired of fighting her own feelings. On the other hand, he couldn't even care to notice her and that would never lead the conversations to something more than a mere friendship. During the exams often Druv called up Roshni to clear doubts. Sometimes Roshni had to teach concepts over calls and in the college library after the exam. She obviously knew nothing about him except that he needed help studying and was not that bad.

Semester results were put up in the college notice board and both Roshni and Druv were finding each other's.

On finding Roshni in the crowd Druv shouted "Roshni! You scored 95% congratulations!" Roshni turned around and made her way to Druv

"Did you see yours? You scored 85%." "Thank you it was all because of you", said Druv.

Roshni smiled, "you're welcome".

Making someone happy and helping them out gave the biggest happiness to Roshni so that actually made her day beautiful.

The next day in college Roshni overheard a group of people talking that Druv and Nandini broke up. She went to sleep early the night before and it suddenly struck her mind that she had 5 missed calls from Druv. She didn't call back in the morning because she would probably meet him in college. Hearing this made her worried that Druv must be hurt.

She hastily walked into the classroom and saw Druv sitting on his place with his head down. Before she could walk towards him, she heard Natasha calling her. Natasha and Meghna knew that Druv and Roshni talked but they had no clue that they were good friends now or maybe just friends and in order to keep her feelings hidden she didn't want to tell them so she walked towards Natasha instead.

"Roshni, Druv and Nandini broke up and you know what the reason was?"

"What?" she tried to look surprised so that she doesn't have to explain herself.

"They broke up because Nandini got to know that Druv had been having two girlfriends apart from Nandini outside college and all this time he had been cheating on her" said Meghna.

Everything that Manasvi told raced through Roshni's mind. Somehow Roshni also started believing that Druv can just play with the feelings of girls. What hurt Roshni the most was that maybe Druv stared at her and gave her attention because he is good at just playing around with everyone. Nandini was not a close friend of Roshni so she could never console her neither could she warn her without evidence in the past.

Moving to her seat she could not help but notice that Druv hadn't been speaking much and getting to know all this about him she was thinking whether she should stay away from him or not because she feared that he may play with her feelings too.

***

"Druv are you ok?", Roshni asked she couldn't stand leaving her friend alone and somewhere she felt that he wasn't wrong. Maybe he should be given the benefit of doubt too. She didn't ask him whether it was true or not she just wanted to be there for him that is what her heart wanted and so did she.

"Yeah I guess so", his face looked pale. The look in his face made Roshni want to comfort him but before she could say anything the lecturer was standing in front of her and she realized that the class had begun.

That night she didn't sleep. No matter how much she wanted, Roshni could not forget the sadness that she saw on Druv's face.

She could not see him hurt. Maybe Druv was not her boyfriend but she had started caring too much for him. Seeing him hurt and being there for him when he had been falling was becoming a tough job for her especially because her feelings were hurting her now. She was not a girl who would confess her feelings and she already feared rejection. As soon as her eyes filled with tears her phone rang. It was Natasha. She quickly wiped off her tears and answered the call.

"H..ell..o" hearing Roshni's voice Natasha got to know that she had been crying.

"Roshni what is wrong? Will you tell me since the past two days you seem so lost and now I feel as if you just cried." Roshni could not hide it anymore she told Natasha how she is in a tough place where she has to be there for Druv also but prevent her feelings from growing. Roshni had been hurt a lot and her heart was scared to fall for anyone so scared that she cried.

Natasha had sensed that Roshni liked Druv by the way she looked at him but she didn't say anything because she thought that may have perceived it wrong, "Roshni gather yourself up I got you. You got to be strong what if aunty saw you crying she'll get tensed na. And about Druv, it is your decision as to what you should do but I suggest you not to do anything that will hurt you."

"Hmm. I don't want to talk right now. Can we please talk tomorrow" Roshni said. She didn't speak much and went to bed after the call.

Seeing Roshni enter the class next day Meghna got up from her seat and hugged her. Roshni figured it out that Natasha told her everything.

"It will be alright I got you", she said.

"We got you! And no matter what decision you take we'll be there" came Natasha's voice from behind Meghna.

Seeing her friends care for her so much Roshni smiled, "thank you guys. You are the best."

"Yeah we know that" Natasha winked at her. Spending the day with her besties made her heart feel at ease.

Two weeks had passed and Roshni hadn't talked to Druv she tried her best to maintain distance. Druv didn't try to talk to Roshni too. In fact, he didn't try to talking to anyone at all and once a rumour had spread that Druv had cut his hand for Nandini, just because she had told him to do so. At first Roshni thought it was the truth and that made her hate Nandini more because it was madness not love. She knew that a person who loves you can never harm you. But eventually she realized that it was just a rumour. But anyhow all she was determined to do was stay away from him as much as she could.

Roshni had talked to her dad she had been missing him a lot but her dad was busy with his business he had said that he may take a week or two more to be able to finish his work and come home.

CHAPTER 3

COLOURS OF THE SPIRIT

A camping trip to Spiti valley, Himachal Pradesh had been organised by their college for all the students of the commerce background. Natasha's parents were not allowing her to go but when Roshni and Meghna requested her mother and assured her that she would call often, they were granted the permission.

Roshni had been very excited about the trip because it was the first time she was going to go on a two day trip with her friends. She rang the bell of her house and as soon as her mom opened the door she hugged her mom

"Mummm.. Guess what Natasha is also coming with us. I am finally going to go out with my best friends. I am so happy." She felt the warmth of her mother's smile through the hug.

Roshni told her mom to pack her favourite cookies and a little lunch and snacks for her and headed to her room for packing. Spiti valley was in the foothills of Himalayas so it would be probably cold there. Roshni packed her favourite overcoat and all the other woollen clothes.

"Roshni don't forget to bring your camera" Meghna's voice echoed in her memory. Her friends always knew the stuff she would forget, they really did get her.

It was a pleasant day and the assembly hall was crowded with about twenty five students. The number of people who were going for the trip was lesser than expected.

"All of you should now go and board the bus", an announcement was made and all the students walked to the ground of the college.

Meghna and Natasha sat together and Roshni sat infront of them.

"May I?" Druv's voice startled Roshni.

"Yeah sure", she removed her bag on the seat beside her.

"So how are you?" Druv asked.

"I am fine and I am excited. But how are you? You don't look fine" as Roshni said that her eyes trailed behind Druv and she could see Nandini staring at them. Roshni was the last person who wanted to get involved in their matters and seeing Nandini glare at her made her uncomfortable.

"Druv I actually had some work with Andrew so if you don't mind can I please go and sit beside him." Before Druv could speak

Roshni took her seat near the window beside Andrew. Andrew was a good guy and welcomed her beside him in a very funny way which made Roshni laugh.

The roads that lead to the valley were treacherous and sometimes freaked some students out. Roshni had her earplugs on and the coolness of the wind made her wish that the journey goes on. The beautiful landscapes caught her attention. Sometimes the roads were blocked due to the local shepherds. The mountains were covered with snow and there was melted ice travelling down the glaciers. The bus had stopped near a tea stall in the corner of the road for a little while where everyone had some hot tea and snacks. After they resumed the journey the usual chit chat had calmed a little and most of the people fell asleep.

***

"Roshni wake up", Andrew's voice whispered and Roshni's eyes fluttered. After a moment she realized that she had fallen asleep too and it had been about an hour. Looking out of the window she saw that the bus had stopped and their destination was right outside. Looking to her right she saw Andrew leaning on her which made her jerk back and she startled.

"Whoa relax girl. Come out of the bus now."

Roshni laughed and got up from her seat. Andrew made a gesture allowing her to get down from the bus before him.

All the tents were already in place and Meghna and Natasha were sitting outside on the chairs waiting for Roshni. The valley was magnificent, it had the lake Chandra which reflected the light of the setting sun. The authorities provided them with the refreshments and as they had been very tired, they all went to their tents early. Meghna, Roshni and Natasha had got their sleep in the bus so they stayed up till late gossiping and talking.

"Roshni all I want to tell you is just be strong ok and it may not be easy to let go of Druv but you have to", Natasha said.

"Yeah I know thinking about being with him or hoping something will only hurt me even more."

"Aww.. Sweetie we will always be with you", Meghna hugged Roshni. " Me too", Natasha joined the hug. Seeing these two girls with her Roshni got the biggest strength.

"Guess what?", Natasha pulled out.

"What?"

"Nitish proposed to me." Natasha said with obvious excitement in her voice.

"OMG really? That is great news. Tell us all about it. How? When?", Roshni said.

Nitish and Natasha had been best friends since 3 years and she had liked him since a year. He was studying in JC College too along with Manasvi of course. This was the biggest happiness Natasha could have got as of now. Hearing such great news made Roshni forget about everything and she heard Natasha out till the very end before they fell asleep.

Roshni was awakened by the tweeting of the birds. She went out of the tent and stretched and yawned while looking at the landscape. Then her eyes caught site of Druv who was standing right behind her.

"Since when have you been watching me?" she said embarrassed.

"Since the time you were stretching and scratching your head like a lazy girl", Roshni was flushed. Her cheeks turned pink.

Druv laughed, "You don't have to be embarrassed you looked cute. Good morning by the way" he said walking towards her.

"Good morning. So you enjoying this place haan?" he said

"Yeah! After all it is the first time I came out on a trip for two days and so far like this that too to such a beautiful place" Roshni said.

"Really? This was the first time you came out on such a trip? How come? Oh yeah I forgot how can aunty let a precious gem like you outside the house that easily", he winked.

"Stop flirting. I hate flirts." Druv's expression changed and as soon as he was about to apologize.

Roshni laughed, "Kidding baba."

Seeing Roshni laugh Druv didn't feel pissed at all. "Anyway I should go wake up my friends now."

She headed to the tent.

"Guys wake up we have to go for trekking today gather all the necessities", Meghna and Natasha took half an hour to wake up and they started packing their bags, ate some snacks and all the students set out for trekking. New things and places always amused Roshni.

***

After a few hours of trekking, they all sat down to take some rest. "Wow man this is so adventurous!" Natasha said. Natasha always wanted to do things like trekking, paragliding, mountain climbing. And now that she got a chance for it she was on cloud nine. After a few more hours all the students returned back to the valley by jeeps.

In the evening all of them took rest and had coffee. "It was real fun today", said Andrew while coming towards the three girls.

"Yeah exactly!", said Natasha.

"So what else now?" asked Andrew.

"I think we should just go and sleep the day had been tiring", Meghna said.

"Sleep? No way. Maybe we'll…" after a short pause he said "let's play a dare game." Before anyone could say anything Andrew announced "Hey guys, all of you come and sit around the camp fire let's play a dare game." Some people agreed some were being insisted finally they all settled down.

"Let's see I am going to select people and one of them will be telling the dare and the other will have to do it. I will point finger at any two people and my eyes will be closed which will be a fair play." Everyone agreed and the game begun.

Krutika got the first dare. She was to slap the person who she hated the most and she ended up slapping Harry her best friend. Woooo everyone started making weird noises to make him feel embarrassed. Druv was given a dare by Mindy to play the guitar.

Hearing him play, Roshni felt happy she closed her eyes to feel the music. The atmosphere turned serine and calm after Druv played. She wondered if it became better because it was him or was he playing that well too. It became so soothing that she felt like sleeping and had already yawned 5 times in the past few minutes.

***

Natasha and Meghna were grinding Roshni between them in sleep which is why Roshni wasn't able to sleep. Frustrated, Roshni went out of the tent for some fresh air. The sky had been dark with few twinkling stars and the moon dimly illuminating the sky. Roshni took a deep breath and exhaled. Looking towards the right she saw a figure sitting near the lake. Going a little closer she saw it was Druv. He sat quietly looking at the sky it seemed as if he was praying. Roshni approached him and said in a soft voice "Hey.. You are not yet asleep?"

"Hmm.. I couldn't sleep because of certain things. Tell me why you aren't asleep?" Druv asked.

"Meghna and Natasha were literally squeezing me in between", he smiled.

"What happened? What is it that is bothering you so much?" Roshni asked.

Druv didn't reply he just looked up at the sky and sighed.

"I did nothing to hurt Nandini she hurt me but no one believes that." He said in desperation.

"I believe you Druv" Roshni wondered if she was thinking before speaking or not. Not knowing why she trusted him so much and how those words left her mouth.

"But you also avoided me today in the bus." he continued.

"Oh that. I had to actually change my place because Nandini was glaring at me and I don't want to come in between you guys. Maybe she will come back to you", Roshni said.

"Roshni, she won't and even if she does I am not taking her back, me and Nandini are over now she hurt me and I have my own reasons. She was the one cheating and created a hoax out of it. She found me as a perfect target and just because I look good, the fact that I cheated looks more believable to people anyway" he said desperately trying to look for consolation.

Roshni didn't ask any further questions she didn't want him to feel uncomfortable. The night had turned chillier and Roshni clenched her fists because of the cold. It was surprising that Druv noticed it and asked if she wanted his jacket.

"No. Thank you but I think I should head to sleep I am really tired", she stood up.

"Okay. Goodnight."

"You go and sleep too don't think about stuff we need to wake up early and leave tomorrow. Goodnight."

***

Roshni turned around and hugged her pillow. Her heart wanted to stay there beside Druv but she had to leave that place.

Talking to Druv only made her feel more for him. She could see that he trusted Nandini and as they were not together for long their bond wasn't strong enough so it was easy for him to let go of her but it hurt him a little she saw in his eyes. Maybe she could not be with him but she always wanted to be a person who set his soul free and who he could rely on.

The next day early in the morning they all boarded the bus and returned home by the evening.

Roshni rang the doorbell and there was no answer. She took out spare keys and opened the door. Her mom was sleeping. She quietly unpacked and rearranged her cupboard and prepared green tea for her mom. Soon her mom was awake and was so pleased to see her daughter making green tea for her.

"How was your trip my baby?"

"It was great mom", she said hugging her mom.

"I missed you so much someday dad, you and me will also go there you will love it." Roshni was exactly like her mom so she knew exactly what her mom would like.

"Sure, we will" her mom said sipping her tea. Roshni quickly asked for a minute and took out a shawl from her bag. She had brought the shawl for her mom when the bus had stopped while coming home. Her mom was surprised "Thank you my bacha. It is so beautiful".

As soon as Roshni thought about her dad her phone rang and it was him. "Daddy.. I miss you when will you be returning come home fast na". "Calm down sweetie I may take a day or two I'll be there soon. By the way when did you return home, I told you to inform me when you reach." "Sorry dad I forgot" Roshni said. Roshni explained everything to her dad and talked for about an hour before going to sleep.

CHAPTER 4

BIRTHDAY GIRL

Roshni took the pillow and covered her ears to prevent the ringing of her cell phone to be heard. It didn't stop ringing so she finally got up and sat on her bed irritated. It was Natasha. She saw that it was still dark. She wondered why she was calling so late at night.

"Hello", Roshni answered the call.

"Hey sweetie, Happy Birthday! I wish you always stay happy like this. May god bless you." As soon as she heard Natasha's excited voice she realized that she hadn't realized that it was her birthday. She relaxed and smiled, "Thank you so much." Before she could speak more, she got a call waiting from Meghna. At the same time there was a knock on her room door. She kept Natasha on hold and opened the door. Her mom hugged her and gave her blessings. After that she received a call from her dad and told Natasha and Meghna that she'll call back in sometime. She talked to her dad and told him to bring her, her favourite chocolates as a birthday gift when he comes after a few days.

"I wish you were here today daddy. I miss you", she said. "I'll be there in a few days have patience my strong girl." He said before hanging up. She talked to Natasha and Meghna on conference for a few minutes and then went back to sleep.

The next morning when Roshni woke up she found that her mom had cooked her favourite food for breakfast. She was happy like a little kid this trend was followed since she was really small but the only person missing was her dad. She really wished he was there with them. She picked up her bag.

"Ma, I may be late today because my friends probably have plans for me" she left her house.

Seeing Roshni, Meghna shouted "Happy Birthday!" without realizing that the entire class got to know that it was Roshni's birthday because of her. Meghna hugged Roshni and gave her a small packed box.

"What is it?" Roshni asked.

"See for yourself" Meghna replied.

Roshni unpacked the box and found a beautiful wind chime in it. She squeaked with excitement. "Oh my god! This is so beautiful."

"You like it?" Meghna asked.

"Like it? I love it. This is so beautiful." Natasha covered Roshni's eyes from behind and allowed her to guess who it is. Once Roshni guessed Natasha hugged her "Happy Birthday bestie!" she said. Roshni smiled "you sure think I am a fool. Who else do you think has the courage to cover my eyes that way" Roshni said.

"Oh dear lord, Lady Don!" Andrew came from behind. They all laughed. Roshni gave a look "whatever" she said and shook her head. She tried being that way and giggled.

"Happy birthday to you, Roshniii.." Andrew sang in a funny voice. Roshni laughed. "Thank you so much" she said.

As soon as it was recess Roshni's classmates started wishing her. Roshni then went to the staff room to take blessings from her teachers. All the teachers had played a very important role in making Roshni good in studies. They all loved her and she respected her teachers too.

"Roshni!" she heard Druv's voice and turned to look at him "Happy Birthday!" He pulled out his hand from his pocket.

"Thank you" Roshni smiled but she didn't take his hand.

"Oh come on it is just a handshake" For an old college romantic like Roshni he didn't know what it meant but just because she didn't want to explain she shook hands with him. His hands seemed to fit perfectly into hers and it felt warm and comfortable.

"So where is the treat?" he asked.

"Umm.." Before she could speak Natasha popped up between them and kept her hand around Roshni's shoulders.

"She won't give you a treat mister, she is our friend" she said.

Druv laughed "oh really Roshni?" he said.

"No no it is not like that" she stammered.

"See she is stammering which means she is not really agreeing with you" Natasha said. Natasha and Druv argued for a bit and Roshni stood there amused by the way they kept on going.

"Guys I am going to treat both of you!" Roshni said and pulled Natasha who was still darting at Druv.

Natasha, Meghna, Druv and Roshni headed to McDonalds. The plan was for pizza but Roshni didn't like pizza, except for what her mom made. "I would like one McAloo Tikki" Roshni said "same for me" Meghna said. Natasha's phone rang and when she was checking the caller id Roshni and Meghna peeped into her phone and started teasing her. It was Nitish. Natasha blushed and excused herself.

"Her boyfriend?" Druv lip synced looking at Roshni and she nodded and he smiled.

"Roshni I need to talk to you about something important. Meghna will you please excuse us" he winked at her. "Yeah sure." Druv and Roshni went out of McDonalds.

"I talked to Nandini. She is committed to some other guy." Druv said.

"What? I mean all this while it was she who had been cheating on you and playing around?"

"Yeah" Druv said "I knew it somewhere I felt that you didn't do anything, that you were not wrong" Roshni said feeling a little ray of hope for them but refrained from smiling.

"Thank you Roshni, for being a good friend of mine" he said. Roshni smiled.

"I'll always be there for you. And please don't worry. Whatever is meant to happen will find its way to you and don't let yourself be sad because of a girl like her." She said.

"Hmm yeah I won't" he said. There was silence. Druv's face turned pale again. Seeing him hurt and worried about his image she wanted to hug him and tell him that she'll stand by him even if no one does. "Hey… It is going to be fine" Roshni said.

Druv sat down in a bench nearby and Roshni joined him. He looked into her eyes.

"Roshni please stay by my side. I may turn out to be a complicated and unpredictable person…." Roshni interrupted "Shhh.. It is okay I'll always be there that is what true friends are for right? And if you ever need me just give a call or text me." She said.

"And I know that no matter how a person is he/she is always good because everyone has a heart right?" she continued "you know Druv I have been always hurt and left alone by my friends and I know how it is to lose you guys so you can trust that I won't leave you guys. If I ever find new friends also I will never forget you guys, especially you." She said. As soon as those words left her mouth she realized what she just spoke. Druv stared at her. Her eyes fluttered and she didn't look at him. Before he could question her why she added 'especially you' she said. "I think we should head inside Meghna is alone" she said and stood up and walked without looking at him.

As she walked away Druv stared and smiled. The smile came unexpectedly and he wondered why he was happy that Roshni added 'especially you' in her sentence.

"Wow" Roshni became speechless. The entire time during which Druv and she were talking outside Natasha had come back and along with Meghna she arranged the table with chocolates and Roshni's favourite cake. Roshni loved surprises and having friends who loved her so much was more than enough for her. "Thank you" she glanced at them. "This means so much to me".

She blew the birthday candles while the others sang happy birthday in chorus. She ate the first piece of cake herself and giggled. Druv could not resist her cuteness and he took some cream from the cake and applied it on her cheeks. She looked at him and their eyes met. Her world seemed to stop for a while the depth of his eyes was far beyond those of the oceans. She got awe struck and could not speak even though she wanted to break the silence. Her heart beats fastened and for a while she forgot everything.

"Guys" Meghna shouted and when the realization struck upon Druv and Roshni about where they were, they got embarrassed and they blushed. Meghna and Natasha started making hooting noises.

On returning home, Roshni got the most amazing surprise. When she entered her house she saw her dad sitting on the couch. She got so happy that she threw her bag and hugged her dad. "I missed you so much" she said. She pulled away and asked "you said you will take some time to come here" she said "I said that to give you a surprise of course" he walked to his room and bought her birthday present. It was a guitar.

Roshni wanted to have a guitar and learn how to play one since she was a child and now she had her dream come true right in front of her. "Thank you so much dad. This is the best birthday gift I could ever get. I love you so much" she said. Her dad smiled. They only thing that Roshni's parents wanted was for her to be happy they never told her to study or achieve anything they just wanted her to live and enjoy her life. Roshni took out the guitar and randomly started playing some chords. Although she didn't have a guitar she had learnt how to play it a little by her friends and internet.

Roshni went to her favourite restaurant for dinner with her parents. She ordered American corn pepper salt and enjoyed the evening with her parents. Her dad told them about his trip and Roshni went on talking about everything she hadn't told her dad about college. (Except Druv. He was just introduced as a new friend). After a long time they three laughed together and Roshni's mom was happy too.

It was Roshni's eighteenth birthday. She didn't expect anything great to happen but the day turned out to be one of the best days of her life. She usually didn't have any friends to celebrate her birthday with and today there were Meghna and Natasha. She got the best surprises for the first time in her life. As she lay on her bed she thanked god for the wonderful day. Although she made each day worth living and loving, this day was special. She had held Druv's hand for the first time and as they shook hands their eyes met. Things were beginning with Druv and her feelings were taking a faster pace. He was not the kind of guy Roshni would like but she got strangely attracted to him and his presence made her happy unknowingly. His hand was warm and she held it for once she felt that now that he was in her life she felt positive that things from now on will turn out to be for the best. She felt happy that Druv relies on her and shares everything with her. She didn't want to own him she just wanted to be the person who sets his heart free for now. She wondered if Druv doubted about her feelings and wondered why her feelings started to show up infront of him. It may turn out to be more difficult to be around him without displaying her feelings. Her dad was back and she could imagine how happy and relieved her mom would be. Her mom didn't say anything but Roshni knew everything of how much her mom missed her dad. The people around her were now happy and things seemed to be falling into place as her heart hoped for the best. This bought peace to her mind and slowly the shutters of her eyes fell and she had a deep and peaceful sleep.

CHAPTER 5

FEAR OF LOSS

"I'll be right there" Roshni said panicking, she hung up the phone. Her legs felt weak and she had to hold the chair to prevent herself from falling. She wiped her tears carelessly and gathered herself up. She took the car keys and rushed to the parking lot. It was dark and her mind was racing. She didn't even realize that she had been driving because his thoughts had flooded all her mind.

She finally pulled the break. The car came to a halt. There it was his house she stood there and stared at it for a moment wondering what she would see the next moment. She felt weak and shivered as she hurried to the door. She pulled the main door open.. "Druv, Druv" she screamed with her weak and scared voice but her voice didn't sound as strong as it would. There was no response from him. She brisked forward and saw his bracelet on the floor near his room while the door was ajar. She pushed the door open horrified at what she may see next. He was laying there on the bed beside his blood stained pillow. She stopped breathing for a moment and was shocked at the site of blood. It was his soft moan that made her come back to the present, she briskly moved towards him and took out her hanky. She wiped his nose with her shivering hands. She trembled and her tried to close her eyes for the sight was too scary to look at.

Looking into his eyes hurt her even more. He held her hand and made her look at him.

She couldn't control her tears and choking in her tears said "I won't let anything happen to you."

***

Roshni suddenly jerked and sat up on her bed. It was just a dream she kept reassuring herself again and again so that she calms down. She carelessly wiped the sweat in her neck and forehead. When she started breathing a little calmer, she walked to the dining table, poured herself a glass of water and sat down.

The dream had felt real. She feared losing him more than anyone she thought. This feeling was something new it wasn't like those of normal crushes she had. This was something she hadn't felt before and she wasn't able to understand anything. On one side she felt like staying away from him and wanted to believe that he was bad and on the other hand her heart wanted to trust him. Every person has a heart she thought so maybe he does not break hearts. Maybe people have been spreading rumours about him because that's what happens to popular people in colleges. That is what people who want to bring you down try to do because they don't have the courage to be toxic to your face or face their own reality. She could trust Nandini if she wanted but as a friend she would be stupid to not put her trust in Druv because he obviously seems to care more about her. Maybe Nandini has some problem with Druv and didn't want to take the blame for it.

***

"What happened Roshni?" Roshni was awakened by Meghna's voice. "Why are you so sleepy today the classes are about to begin" Natasha said. "I wasn't able to sleep properly last night" she said and coughed. She saw a hand offering water. It was Druv. "You look tired and how come this coughing?" he asked. "She coughs every time she is tensed." said Meghna. Roshni drank some water and wondered how clueless and alive he looked after the nightmare she experienced. She felt relieved and sighed.

After recess Roshni felt weak and feverish. Maybe she shouldn't have come to college or maybe if her heart would be ok with not seeing Druv after that horrible dream; she would have stayed home and rested.

"Hey, want to bunk this class? Let's go somewhere else you'll feel more sick if you stay here any longer" Druv winked. She gave the obvious smile of the excitement to do something daring every time she felt down "Sure."

"So we are going to get out of the class now" Roshni looked at Megha and Natasha for their approval, she wasn't going anywhere without these two. Druv saw the teacher entering. He held Roshni's hand and pulled her. Her eyes widened when she saw the situation and she knew she had to run before they got caught. They both were running out of the class before Natasha or Meghna made up their minds to.

Roshni looked beside her and heard the sound of Druv's magical laugh. His hand in hers had a strong grip and they ran as if they had left the whole world behind them. Their hearts felt happiness and they looked at each other laughing and running like kids. It was like a dream come true. Little things like this stole away her heart. She didn't want to stop running she wanted to just go on and was secretly hoping for Natasha and Meghna to not make their way out. In a while, she was out of the college main entrance and then Druv stopped and stood there panting and smiling.

"So where do we go now? It is just two of us poor Natasha and Meghna were left behind" Druv said. Roshni suddenly felt her vision get blurry and the world spinning. "I don't know I'll just head home soon because I am not really feeling well" she said feeling guilty about being happy that her friends were left behind. "Okay then let's just go and sit somewhere." Druv said. She didn't have anything in mind and knew that being with him was anyway going to take away the unnecessary stress, so maybe she won't feel so ill after all. "okay" she said still holding his hand tighter like she drew strength from him.

***

The coffee shop was scarce for people due to the glimmering sun and it was the perfect day because Roshni didn't like crowds.

"So tell me about your hobbies" Druv said.

"Writing is my passion apart from that I love singing and reading too. What are yours?" Roshni said casually munching on the complementary cookies.

"I actually play football. I have always wanted to be a football player. I have been recently selected for the state level." He said. The excitement in his voice helped Roshni predict how much he probably loved it. "Ronaldo and David Beckham are my favourite players and football is my first love." As he went on Roshni patiently heard him out. Although the subject didn't interest her much, the excitement with which he talked did all the magic.

"Did I get you bored?" he asked. "Nope" she said and ordered a cold coffee.

"Do you like reading?" she asked.

"No only football" he laughed.

"I started reading when I was in class eight and my favourite series is the House of Night. It is the most beautifully written book and it is totally unputdownable." She said.

"I'll read that for sure if I get a chance." He said

"You don't have to" she said.

"But I want to" he said with a steady gaze which made her blush.

"Where are you from?" she asked changing the topic, trying hard to not blush anymore.

"I am from Dubai. I was born there and spend like five years there." He replied. She nodded while sipping her coffee.

Roshni again felt herself getting dizzy and blinked to see if she can clear her vision.

"Hey, are you ok?" Druv asked getting up and moving beside her.

"Yeah I am. But I think I should head home now. Could you book me a cab?" She said feeling ashamed of suddenly getting sick in front of him and embarrassing herself. Druv immediately booked a cab for her and helped her outside the café.

"I think I should come with you" he offered.

"No I am fine. I don't want you to" she said before she left for home.

Druv waved at her as the cab moved. He got worried about her. He liked being with Roshni and being around her made him more comfortable than with anyone else. Her eyes spoke a lot he felt. There was pain deep down them and he felt like protecting her. She understood him and he smiled with the happiness. As his smile emerged he wondered if he had started liking her. Because seeing her alone or upset was the last thing he could bear he thought. He was already worried about her health. Somewhere he had started to fear losing her too.

***

"Where is Roshni?" Natasha asked as she and Meghna met Druv at the college entrance.

"She wasn't well so she has headed home. Don't worry, nothing serious she just needs some rest" he said.

***

Roshni lay down on her bed. "What happened my daughter." Her mom asked "Nothing mom I just want to rest I feel ill" she said. Her mom made some hot soup for her and comforted her. Roshni slowly sipped down the soup feeling its warmth realising how well her mom knew exactly what she needed.

"I think I will sleep for a bit ma" she said and hugged her mom before sleeping.

***

As Druv looked at Roshni's picture he smiled. 'God knows how suddenly this girl came to my life.' He thought. Like a rush of wind in the sunny day Roshni had come into his life making him feel relieved and comfortable. He closed his eyes and he could see her smiling face. Whenever a person looked at Roshni they felt happiness. She was a jovial girl they said and that was her real charm.

***

"What? How?" Roshni's eyes fluttered open in her sleep as she heard her mom's voice. She could sense the panic in her voice and she immediately realized that something was wrong. She removed her blanket and walked briskly from her bed.

She saw her mom sitting at the dining table. She looked depressed.

"Mom what happened?" she asked. Her mom looked at Roshni and there was hurt in her eyes. Roshni got worried and held her. "Tell me ma what happened?"

"Your maternal granddad is in the hospital we need to leave for Kolkata soon." Her dad said and went to the kitchen to get water.

"Here drink this" he said to Roshni's mom offering her water.

"What? How come he is in the hospital what happened?" Roshni asked.

"He wasn't well since the past one week but we didn't think that for that he will have to be admitted in the hospital" her dad replied. Roshni's mom burst into tears.

"Mom don't worry nothing will happen to granddad he will be fine" Roshni controlled her tears because she knew this was the time to be strong.

"Dad, you and mom should take the earliest flight. I will handle everything here" she said.

Roshni had never lived alone at home and barely knew how to cook but seeing Roshni stand up and say something so brave her mom smiled.

"My daughter has grown up." She said through her tears.

Roshni smiled "Trust me mom. Granddad will be fine. Now go see him I'll take care of everything here I promise" she hugged her mom.

Roshni booked two flight tickets which was at 7pm. They had only two hours to pack up and leave. Roshni quickly helped her dad pack the bags.

"Are you sure you will be able to live alone here?" her dad asked.

"Yes dad don't worry about me." She said as she bid them a goodbye.

***

Roshni sank on the sofa and sighed with sadness. Her mom's face was so pale. Her granddad was in his late 80s and they could lose him anytime she knew. Roshni's family consisted of only her parents. The others in their family had always left them alone in the tough times. Although she had never spent more than a few days with her granddad she felt sad. She could imagine how much her mom was hurt. She walked to the kitchen and poured herself a glass of water. Her parents knew she hated being alone but somehow she felt strong today. She opened her diary and began to write.

"There is power in pain, kindness in the darkest souls and beauty in the night. All a person needs is the right eyes and right mind to figure it all out. The world is blinded by physical beauty and materialism. But the one who can go beyond the two can enjoy life in every single way. The beauty of nature and the coolness of wind, the warmth of the sunshine and the peace of the moonlight can be understood and endured by the purest of the souls. When the innocence of a person turns into maturity of the same. When the love for nature is more important than the love for mankind and the love for hearts is more important than the love for faces. That's when you know life happened.

Problems don't define people, how they handle the problems define them. It takes courage to move on when life throws problems at us. We break down yeah, we do. But once we decide and make up our minds we need to get up and walk. We need to live and love like no one else did. We need to achieve and succeed. We need to prove ourselves by awakening the strength inside us. What is meant to stay will stay. So we need to let go and breathe because beautiful things are coming our way. Life is not over it is just the beginning."

She wiped her tears and closed her diary. Writing made her heart feel at ease.

Just then Meghana called. She took her call and started explaining everything that was happening.

"No Meghna you don't have to come here I can handle everything" Roshni said.

"What do you mean you'll handle everything I know you hate being alone" Meghna said.

"It is ok my parents will be back in a day." She said. "I am not listening to anything I'll be there in sometime" Meghna said before she hung up.

Roshni heard the dialler sound before she could speak. She smiled. She knew that her friends will never leave her alone. It was good that Meghna was coming at least she would be cheered up. On the other hand being alone with her thoughts can only make her think about her granddad.

After an hour Roshni heard the doorbell ring. It was Meghna and Natasha.

"You came too?" Roshni got excited.

"Yeah baby! Let's have a pyjama party today." Natasha said and barged into the house. Roshni laughed and let Meghna in.

CHAPTER 6

TO EXPECT THE UNEXPECTED

Roshni and Natasha started the movie 'Dead poet's society' while Meghna poured the soft drinks. They just got the opportunity of a lifetime to party, they were not going to miss it for anyone.

"I don't want to watch this stupid movie' Meghna said as she sat on the sofa.

"Watch it you are going to love it" Roshni said.

"Fine" Meghna said.

"See it is two for one so we win" Roshni said she winked at Natasha.

After five minutes Meghna agreed to watch it with a bet that if she didn't like the movie then the two others will treat her.

By the time they completed the movie, they were all dozing off in the sofa.

****

The next day the doorbell rang continuously. Roshni woke up and took a glimpse at the watch. It was 4am in the morning. Her eyes widened and she realised the possibility of a robber or someone coming. She started freaking out as the doorbell was ringing continuously. Meghna and Natasha woke up too.

"Who is it at this time?" Natasha asked.

"I don't know. The security guard last night took a leave because his wife was sick so it can be anyone." Roshni said.

"We have to open the door anyway" Meghna said. "It can be someone we know" she added.

"Let's just ignore it. Who is so dumb that he/she will come at 4am in the morning? What if, it is a thief or something?" Roshni said.

After a few seconds they all agreed on opening the door. Natasha took a knife from the kitchen; Roshni had the mop in her hand while Meghna took the broom. They all stood in different directions in front of the door.

Roshni twisted the door knob and opened the door. "bhoo" a voice shouted. The three girls screamed and became alert. Upon realization they all burst out laughing. It was Druv.

Roshni smacked him on his shoulder. "What the hell are you doing here at 4am?" she said. "and freaking us out at this time" Natasha added.

"Roshni wasn't well yesterday and I was worried about her. On the other hand, I got to know you three were partying without me so I thought I should punish you guys for that." He smiled and winked at Roshni.

Roshni wondered how he got to know and then realized that last night Andrew had called her and as he was a really trustable fellow she told him all that was happening.

"That was a really bad prank." Meghna said pissed.

"Haha chill it was just to freak you guys out and trust me it was fun." He laughed.

All of them were sleepy but as Druv was there they decided to watch a movie or some series. The four of them sat on the sofa and started watching F.R.I.E.N.D.S. Roshni sat beside Druv.

"Switch on the fan" Druv said.

"No. it is really cold" Roshni said.

Everyone pretended that they didn't hear her so she ended up bringing a blanket for herself. She was already not really well and stressed out and then she had such morons who were with her because she didn't like being alone but were ok with the fact that she is cold. She decided to call her parents after a few hours and ask about granddad's condition she thought. 'F.R.I.E.N.D.S' was her favourite TV series it was something that made her laugh like a kid even when her life was at its worst place. The other day she had told Druv about it which the reason why he suggested watching it was, probably. It is not that he didn't care although he didn't say anything she could see how worried he was about her that as soon as he got a chance, he came to see her. She didn't want to fight the fact that he was someone who made her heart flutter and she wanted more than to just be friends with him. The fact that he was sitting beside her and had come to see her made her blush. He was worried about her so maybe he has feelings for her too but she knew that she was wrong in thinking so of course most of us think our crushes like us too but that is usually not the case and we end up fooling ourselves. At least her heart was in peace that he was a little happier than before and he had her as a friend who he can share everything with.

"Can you please share your blanket with me" Druv whispered. It made her shudder and before she could say something he made himself comfortable by pulling one side of the blanket over his legs.

She looked to her right. Meghna and Natasha were already asleep beside her on the sofa. They must have been really sleepy especially after someone freaks them out at 4am in the morning. She smiled and wondered what her life would have been without these two idiots.

Roshni then looked at Druv. She watched him. His tiny eyes shuttered down and his lovely eyelashes rested on the crust of his eyes. His face showed the greatest expression of serenity and the warmth of his body soothed her. His peace mesmerized her and made her forget all that had happened.

***

Roshni and Druv woke up hearing 'aww' and clicking sounds. When Roshni's eyes opened she saw Meghna and Natasha staring at them and clicking pictures. She looked to her left and realized that she had been sleeping on Druv's shoulders the entire time. Druv's eyes opened and they both jerked apart embarrassed.

"Hey! Stop clicking pictures" Druv chased after Natasha and Meghna.

"We are not giving it." Natasha shouted as she was running.

"We will show this to Nandini" Meghna laughed.

Roshni came into Natasha's way and got the cell phone from her.

***

"Hello. Mom how is grandpa?" Roshni asked.

"He is better than before Roshni. How is everything there?" her mom asked.

"Everything here is ok mom Meghna and Natasha are going to live here till you come back" she said. Roshni explained all that had happened since the day before and how Druv showed up early in the morning and surprised by how accepting her mother was of him staying over.

"Mom, are you ok?" she asked.

"Yes baby. You don't worry about me grandpa will be back to normal soon too. And we'll probably be home by tomorrow" her mom said.

As Roshni hung up the only thing she wanted was to see her mom and whether she was ok or not. She didn't realize when she had started crying.

"Hey" she looked up to see Druv offering her a hanky. She took the hanky and wiped her tears.

"Are you ok?" he asked.

"Yeah I am fine" she said and turned her head because looking into his eyes would make her want to cry more as hiding her pain would become tougher. Druv kept his hand on her shoulder "it's okay". Everything will be fine. Trust me." He said. Roshni nodded her head and walked to the kitchen.

Druv felt like hugging her. He didn't know why he didn't like that Roshni was sad. It was then that the realization struck upon him that he may have had feelings for her for way longer than just now.

***

"Meghna and Natasha please take care of the house I'll be back in sometime. I need to go and buy some groceries for cooking." Roshni said.

"Yeah ok" they said.

"Hey Roshni I'll join you too. You'll get bored" Druv said and followed her out.

"Here give me these" Druv took the shopping bags from Roshni's hands. She smiled.

"What else should we buy" she thought.

"Chocolates" he said. He remembered that a few hours ago Roshni wanted to have chocolates and so did he.

The four of them started organising the grocery when suddenly Meghna's phone rang. She blushed and walked to the balcony after excusing herself. The rest glanced at each other and laughed.

"Hello" Meghna said "what's up" Andrew said.

"Nothing as you know we are all in Roshni's house arranging the grocery and stuff", she said.

"Oh that is nice" he said.

"So how was your day" she asked.

"It was boring as usual" he said.

"Really if you say your day was boring then what should we say" she laughed.

"Oh common my jokes only work when people are around. Living here in this empty flat is just so disgusting" he said.

"You are never alone all of us are with you only" she said.

"Yeah thank you" he said.

Meghna talked to him for about half an hour.

***

"Who was it?" Roshni stood there looking at her suspiciously.

"Omg! You startled me" Meghna jumped back.

"Nothing it was just a friend" she blushed as she said. Roshni raised her eyebrow

"Really?" she asked.

"Yeah ok fine it was Andrew" she blushed. Roshni smiled

"You like Andrew?" She got excited and walked towards Meghna.

"Umm. Yeah I think so" Meghna said.

"And I think he likes me too he is my best friend" she said.

"That is great" Natasha's excited voice came from behind Roshni. Meghna blushed.

"Bitch! You didn't even tell us about it" she smacked her shoulders.

The two of them teased her for some time and asked about when it all started. Meghna explained to them how it all started when they were at spiti valley. While Roshni slept off in the bus Andrew and Meghna talked about many things and they had a lot in common. Slowly they had turned out to be best friends where they shared all the things with each other. Although they didn't talk much in college because he is usually busy with his other friends, he called Meghna up almost every day to talk to her.

"Oh shit! Druv is alone in the kitchen" Roshni realised that she may have left someone who would burn all food with food and she briskly left the balcony. She saw Druv still trying to figure out which things have to be kept in which place. She sat down beside him

"It's okay thank you I will do the rest" she said and removed his hand.

"No really I want to help" he insisted.

The four of them cooked dinner together. While cooking Roshni and Meghna were covered with flour. Roshni had always wanted to cook with her friends and she finally got a chance.

"Dinner is ready. You guys sit at the dining table I'll serve it for you" Roshni said swooping with a tray of salad. Druv helped her serve dinner and they were all finally full.

After dinner Roshni went to the terrace to get some fresh air. They day had went well and Roshni had somehow managed to go through it. It would have been really tough if her friends weren't there. Druv was really good to her. A complete gentleman. She loved being around him because it made her feel protected. She wanted to be with him. He took care of every little thing about her. She never asked for help but he knew everything before she could speak. She wanted to hold his hand and walk with him to the most beautiful dreams. She wanted to show him the best colours of the world and give him strength, courage and support each moment of his life.

"Hey I got a mat, we can sit here." Druv called out. She turned around and saw him walking towards her.

"Where is Meghna and Natasha?" she asked.

"They are downstairs. They said they had some work." Roshni could understand that their work was to let her and Druv spend some time alone. They are so dead she thought. She sat beside Druv on the mat.

In sometime, they both lay on the mat looking at the sky. There was silence in the night. But the silence out there talked about love. The sky was lit up with the stars and the moon. The theory of love is known to all but those who feel it know that there can never be a more pure feeling she thought. Right now she was lying beside someone who she really loved. She wanted to be there for him and was happy just seeing him smile. The sky was boundless and vast. The beauty of it mesmerized both of them.

"It looks so beautiful" Druv said.

"Hmm. I have never looked at the sky this way. But now seeing it I feel like I am flying. I feel like I am in a whole other world" she said

"I feel like lying here forever and just looking at it." He said

"You know Roshni you are a great girl and you are really strong. Promise me one thing" he looked at her "that you will always be the same." He said.

She looked at him and their eyes locked. "hmm" she nodded.

The two of them lay there for about half an hour when Druv's phone rang. It was his mom.

"I think I should get going now. My mom will get worried" he said.

"Yeah sure." She said. They got up and headed downstairs.

***

"You are leaving?" Natasha asked. "It is good only at least I'll have some peace of mind" Meghna said. Druv laughed.

"You act like my little sister Meghna" Druv said.

"Ya ok whatever" she said. Druv never knew that the person who he just called to be 'like his sister' was the girl who had a crush on him on the very first day but slowly grew to not like him because of what Manasvi told she thought. After a five minutes talk with them Druv bid them a goodbye and left.

"So? How was it?" Natasha winked. Roshni blushed

"Shut up! There is nothing between us" she said as she got the bed ready for sleeping. She had talked to her parents and they were going to return the next day. Although things in her life had turned out to be tough and it messed her up, that one hour with Druv was more than enough to make her day.

"Lie to yourself all you want.." Natasha said walking away.

***

CHAPTER 7

A MOMENT OF LOVE

'When I see you I feel alive. It makes me bloom like a flower and blossom like a tree. The happiness you give me is something no one can give. That happiness only comes when you are happy. Your happiness gives me strength and your smile takes away my breath. Keep smiling because it gives someone life. You may be unaware but you are that someone's soul. She is all she is just because you are around her. I know you care. I feel that you want to but you can't speak out the feelings dwelling in you. But, I don't know why I feel so. All I know is you are my life and you will be. No matter how much you hurt me. I promise I won't leave you alone. And all you need to do is trust me I won't ever let you be hurt.'

Roshni closed her diary.

"Who did you write that for?" Roshni was startled. She saw Druv standing behind her.

"Wh...at..?" she stammered.

"The thing you wrote in your diary. Who do you love?" he asked.

"No one" she said without looking into his eyes as she got up from her seat. She held her diary with her strongest grip in her hand and walked passed Druv to go back to her seat from the last bench of the class.

Druv sat in one of the last benches. Seeing Roshni write something like that he felt uneasy. He wondered who she wrote it for. He wanted that someone to be him. He wanted to be with Roshni. Thinking about the possibility of Roshni liking someone else hurt him. His world lit up when she smiled. She gave her courage and strength like no one else could. He wanted to protect her like a shield and take away all her pain. His feelings were growing rapidly and he feared losing Roshni to someone else now.

"Roshni, will you come for dinner with me tonight?" he asked. Roshni looked up at him and wondered why he suddenly asked such a thing. She wondered if he read whatever she wrote and maybe he got to know that it was written for him so he wanted to question her. Thousands of thoughts and questions took over her mind.

"Hello, Roshni?" Druv waved his hands in front of Roshni's eyes. Roshni came back to her senses

"Why? Is it something important?" she asked.

"I just need a break from these regular schedules and go out with my best friend sometime" he said.

"Yeah ok" Roshni agreed. She felt relieved that it was nothing related to whatever she wrote. He probably didn't read it she thought.

It was the first time she was going out for dinner with a guy. Of course it wasn't a date or maybe it was so Roshni wanted to look good because after all it was Druv who she was meeting. She opened her cupboard and took out her favourite black dress. She had got it as present. She loved the dress because of the colour combination of pink and black and how it perfectly fit her.

Hotel Blue Marine was less crowded probably because it wasn't a weekend.

"You look beautiful" she turned around to see Druv dressed up like a handsome knight.

"You look handsome" she said "and thank you" she said.

"Sorry, I am late" he said.

"It's okay. It has been barely five minutes since I arrived" she said.

"Thank you" Roshni smiled as Druv pulled out the chair for her.

"So, what would you like to have?" he passed on the menu to Roshni.

"How was your day?" she asked.

"It was good" he replied. There was an awkward silence.

" Druv.." He said "yeah I'm listening tell me."

"Why do I feel that something is bothering you? Are you ok?" she asked.

"Do you like someone?" he asked. "I mean yeah I know it is none of my business but can you please tell me?" Roshni was silent she didn't say anything.

"I saw whatever you wrote in that diary" he said. "Oh" Roshni regretted coming out for dinner with him. If he got to know she has feelings for him then it may break their friendship. It would bring awkwardness between them. It was ok if he can't be with her but it would hurt her the most to lose him even as a friend. She knew Druv didn't have any other good friend in college and she wanted to be the person who was by his side. She didn't want him to be hurt just because of her own feelings.

"Druv, I don't like anyone" she said "I wrote it because I felt like writing it. It didn't mean anything and it wasn't for anyone." She completed. Roshni didn't know what else to say she had to save her friendship with him. Druv knew she was lying and she didn't want to tell him anyway he couldn't force her to tell him because it may offend her. The feeling that Roshni is now even hiding stuff from him, bore holes in his heart. He didn't want to risk his friendship but now he felt that it was time she knew. Maybe it will make him lose her forever he thought but he had no other option. He can't let her go with someone else he thought.

"Roshni I want to tell you something." He gathered all his courage to speak. She looked at him. Her heart fluttered as if she knew what was going to come up next.

"I know that it has been six months that I am out of a relationship. I am glad that it is gone. Nandini was never the right girl for me. She never understood me. But I want to confess something.." he said. There was silence. He continued "since the first day of college I felt positivity around you which is why I wanted to be your friend. I tried to talk to you many times but you always gave me short replies and our conversation never lasted for more than five minutes in the beginning." Roshni wondered and realized how he noticed everything. She definitely avoided him for obvious rumours.

"However time did its work and we became really good friends." Roshni just stared at him. He wondered what she was thinking by now she had predicated what he was going to say. "I forget everything when you are close to me. I don't know how. It just happens. You know what? I don't know what you feel for me but I want to tell you one thing always keep smiling. Broken hearts start smiling. A world with darkness lights up. Death turns to life….' He paused laughed and said "metaphorically" and continued "and tears turn into strength and happiness. All this can happen with just one lovely smile from your beautiful lips. I love your smile." Roshni blushed and she couldn't for a moment think that the person she wanted to be with and fell in love with, felt the same way about her.

"Yeah ok I want to propose you this way because you love such things I know" he said.

Roshni wondered how Druv knew her so well. Druv kept his hand on Roshni's hand. Roshni felt butterflies in her stomach as she looked into his eyes. "I love you" he said.

Roshni's heart pounded against her chest and her happiness made her eyes smile. She never thought even in her dreams that Druv would feel for her. Soon Manasvi's words again hit her brain. She didn't completely trust Druv she thought. "Druv, I need some time to decide on it" she said as she picked up her purse. "I need to rush home right now. My mom must be waiting" she said.

As Roshni drove home she could not think of anything but just how beautifully everything happened. It seemed like a dream come true. She blushed thinking about whatever happened but was scared that this was just a path towards destruction. Everyone looks good on the outside, who knows what is going on in his head. But could someone fake something like this? The proposal felt so real. What he said was all that he observed about her and he seemed to know what he was talking about.

***

"My heart is singing songs. My stomach feels ticklish. My legs are willing to dance. My eyes wanting to look at him. Because the love I was longing for is finally mine. I feel strong, energetic and I am filled with zest. Optimism is running down my spine and there is pride in my blood. Yes, after the dark night I am finally entering the dawn. I feel blessed and showered with the wishes of my well-wishers. I am strong enough to keep things to myself and I wish to move forward in my life."

As Roshni wrote this down in her diary, she wondered how suddenly her life has changed. Druv was the person she wanted to be with. Her knight in shining armour, her prince charming whatever people may say. She loved him but she was apprehensive. Maybe Nandini and Druv broke up because Manasvi was right she doubted. Roshni had trusted many people in her past and those people were the ones who hurt her the most. She didn't want to repeat the same mistake, especially after being warned for it. She felt like going and telling Druv everything about her feelings but her mind stopped her. She was perplexed. She didn't want to give up now that he too loved her. She wanted to give it a try for the sake of her heart so that she doesn't regret in future. "I should give it a try. Maybe it is meant to be. Maybe he genuinely likes me. For a relief to my heart I have to. "she said to herself. "If I really love him then I need to trust him in what he is saying. I cant just listen to what the world has to say. I cant be so stupid."

That night Roshni stayed up and wrote a letter for him.

The next day in college Roshni saw Druv staring at her. They didn't speak to each other much. Because she knew that if she tried talking he must be expecting an answer soon. Roshni didn't want to start that conversation before classes ended.

When it was dispersal time, Roshni went to Druv and handed him the letter. Before he could open it, she turned around and walked briskly. She didn't want him to open it in front of her.

Dear Druv,

Rose petals shower on me each time I walk. Birds tweet me good morning with their songs. When I am scared at night your thoughts make me smile. There is a lovely forest of love which gets me deeper lost inside it. There were jingles and songs that played in my ears that remind me of you. I was scared to fall in love and now you got me crazy. I know these days had been tough for you. Some people tell me that I shouldn't trust you but I don't know if they can ever be right but I do trust you. I want to give this a try. I want to give us a try. I don't know if it will work out or not but I promise to try my best on making it work.

Here is a poem I wrote for you.

"You are my precious gem only mine.

You are found nowhere but inside me as my soul,

Your core is pure and beautiful

Your value priceless

One of a kind and only mine

Always and Forever"

I love you too.

Roshni

As Druv was reading the letter he smiled and blushed. Roshni was really good at expressing which made him fall for her more every single time she wrote. She had finally said a yes and he wanted to be with her and never hurt her. She trusted him when no one did and that was what meant the most to him.

***

Roshni turned and tossed in her bed as she could not sleep at night because of the happiness that she got by finally giving a response. That's when suddenly her phone rang. Seeing the caller id made her blush and she accepted it.

"Hello" she heard Druv's voice.

"Hey" she said" how was your day" she asked.

"What do you think? How was it?" he asked. She blushed.

"I don't know.' She replied.

"You made my day wonderful. Thank you" He said.

Roshni's cheeks turned pink. After a small silence she asked "had your dinner?"

"Yeah. You have already started caring a lot about me haan?" he said.

"Stop making me blush so much" she said.

"Do you not want to say anything else?" Druv asked, before hanging up. Roshni knew what he was expecting.

"No" she giggled.

"OK. Then I won't talk to you." He said.

"No no. I love you" she said.

"I love you too" he said "I can't ever live without talking to you. I called you up because I couldn't sleep before talking to you" he said. And the conversation lasted for the entire night.

CHAPTER 8

MILES TO GO

As Roshni opened her Facebook profile the first thing that she saw was that she had been tagged in a post by Druv. She was surprised to see that the post declared that they both (Druv and Roshni) are in a relationship. She scrolled down and saw comments like 'oh my god. When did this happen?' and 'you didn't even tell me' which were probably by his best friends. She wondered that now her entire class, actually half the college knows about their relationship. Roshni believed that a relationship should be kept a secret because the more people know about it the more problems it creates. Because she knew that only few people actually wish for your happiness not all the people. There were few people in her class who liked Druv and she knew about it they will be hurt she thought. But now that the truth was in front of them it was better. She didn't want to tell Druv to do something because it hadn't been even one day that they came together and he may start thinking that she has started complaining already.

Her thoughts were interrupted by her phone. It was Meghna. She knew the reason of the call and realized that she had been so lost thinking about Druv and the proposal that she forgot to even tell her best friends about it.

"You are in a relationship with Druv?" Meghna darted the question as soon as Roshni accepted the call.

"You didn't even tell us" said Natasha. Oh wow they were in a conference she thought.

"Yeah. I am sorry I didn't tell you guys I was just going to tell you..."

"When were you going to tell us? The whole college probably knows before us" Natasha interrupted.

"Anyway leave all that tell me how it was?" Meghna's voice turned from being pissed to a lighter tone which made the other two laugh.

Roshni explained everything to them about how he made the beautiful effort of proposing her by a few poetic lines that he had written himself. Both her best friends were awestruck by how beautiful the proposal was and really happy that finally Roshni found someone to love her exactly the way she wished to be loved. They just wanted her to stay happy.

The next day when Roshni entered the class almost all the people present there started gathering around her asking questions about her relationship out of curiosity. Everyone teased her with his name. She looked away a little and her cheeks grew pink which he usually saw when she was around him. That was the moment when she realized that her heart was happy and her soul no longer longed for its fulfilment. His words made Roshni think only about the present and future. The past seemed distant and forgotten, something which she always wished to do happened in just a matter of few days i.e. the day they became friends.

***

Roshni met Nandini in the washroom. She gave her a glance and avoided the stare.

"Hey Nandini" Reshma said as she entered the washroom. Reshma was Nandini's closest friend from another section. Roshni was not popular in college like Nandini was and her friend circle was limited to Natasha and Meghna. And of course as Nandini was one of the most beautiful girls in college she got that attention from people too. Roshni respected and regarded Nandini as a good person before this day.

"Oh hi" Reshma said as she turned back to Roshni.

"Hi" Roshni said nervously not knowing why she just said that because Reshma didn't even know her.

"Do you know Reshma? Roshni is in a relationship with Druv.." Nandini said as she kept her hand on Reshma's shoulder.

"Yeah of course I do" she replied

"After all Druv found another prey for himself" they laughed.

Roshni clenched her fist in anger. She did not want to get into an argument with them because she was rational enough.

"Which girl is so dumb that she will go with him after all this happened" Nandini added as they both walked out leaving Roshni alone in the washroom.

People hardly knew Roshni in the college but just in one day almost the entire college knew her and they know her as being one girl who chose a characterless guy as her boyfriend. No one really understood her feelings. There was now a new gossip in the air and not only Nandini but she knew what all people will start thinking of her.

***

When Roshni reached home she called up Druv. She told him all that happened in the washroom.

"What? How dare she behave like that with you? I'll talk to her tomorrow" he said.

"No Druv. It's okay. I'll handle all this it is not a big thing. On the other hand, let's not make it big we all know that she is just jealous." Roshni said.

"But Roshni today she said and tomorrow someone else. Why didn't you say something?" he asked.

"I didn't want to get into an argument with someone who will never understand" she said. "If she crosses her limit then I will have speak."

Druv hated it when he got to know that Roshni had to go through so much to be with him, he knew that it would be tougher than imagined. Roshni not only chose Druv but she also chose to stand by him where more than half the college hated Druv for the false rumours.

"Hey.." Roshni knew what his silence meant. "You are with me right? Let me tell you one thing Druv. You are not alone in this fight because now it's our fight. We'll stay together no matter what. I don't care what people say because I know you are with me and I am happy" she said.

"I love you" Druv said. As Roshni heard him her heart skipped a beat and after a pause she replied "I love you too" she smiled.

After a conversation of a few more minutes they slept peacefully. Their souls were one and that's what gave relief to both of them.

***

Roshni woke up with the sound of notification in her phone. It was Druv's.

Druv: Good morning my Shona.

Roshni wondered how she loved the word 'shona' which meant sweet and it seemed so perfect when he used it.

Roshni: Good morning ☺

Druv: Coming to college?

Roshni: It depends on whether I'll get to see you or not

Druv: I miss you. Roshni blushed.

Roshni: I miss you too.

Druv: Come to college fast. Hehe.

Roshni kept her phone aside and went to get ready. It was sweet of Druv to make her day wonderful by just bringing a smile on her face early in the morning.

***

"Hey Andrew! Where have you been, man?" Druv asked as he hoped and sat on one of the tables.

"Nothing bro. I had been sick the past few days." He said

"Sick? How?" Druv asked.

Druv saw Roshni entering the class and she smiled. Andrew saw them exchanging glances and lip syncing. As Andrew had been unwell he knew nothing about what was going on.

"Dude what's up with you two?" he asked.

"You don't know" Vishal said as he joined the conversation.

"Druv and Roshni got committed." He said.

When Andrew again looked at them he saw Druv lip syncing that she looked beautiful and Roshni replied with blushing. Druv got down from the table and went to talk to her. Andrew excused himself and went to the washroom.

"Hey!" Druv said as he slipped his hand down to hold Roshni's hand. Their fingers threaded together and she looked at him and smiled.

"Hey Druv!" Meghna said. "Who gave you the permission to hold my best friend's hand" she said."

Druv lifted their hands up and said "She is my girl now".

"Did you have your breakfast my shona" he turned to Roshni

"Yeah and you?" she asked. "Yeah did".

"Aww you guys" Natasha said as she opened the chocolate in her hand.

"I want that" Meghna said.

Roshni snatched it in the blink of an eye and they laughed. Roshni looked at her friends and Druv. She wondered if this is a dream because everything looked so perfect. She never thought that one day there would be someone who swooped into her life and takes her heart away. She didn't know the mysterious and wonderful ways in which destiny functions. Her friends looked perfectly happy and she wanted to capture their smiles in her heart. Someone said the right thing, 'the best moments are never caught in cameras'.

***

Andrew splashed water on his face continuously and looked at the mirror. "Druv and Roshni got committed" Vishal's voice echoed in his ears. He had been sick and so much happened in one day he thought. Druv didn't deserve Roshni. Since they had gone to the trip in spiti valley Andrew had begun to like Roshni. She was a sweet girl with a great sense of humour. Being close to her and talking to her made him feel happy and positive. Her smile was worth a million dollar he thought. She was the most beautiful girl for him and he wanted to be with her. He had loved sitting beside her and talking to her. Although presently Druv and Andrew became good friends Andrew didn't want

Roshni to be hurt because of him. He didn't want to believe in the possibility of Druv being a good guy and that he had gotten Roshni's heart. He couldn't see them together. He had become Meghna's best friend to find out more and get closer to Roshni and he had no clue about all this happening. He wished he could do something. He wished he met Roshni the way Druv did. The only thing that came to Andrew's mind was that he should confess his feelings. He didn't think about the consequences. He wiped his face with a handkerchief and walked out of the washroom.

Andrew saw Natasha, Meghna, Roshni and Druv talking and laughing together. Seeing Roshni and Druv holding hands he felt hurt. His heart felt holes in it.

"Roshni I need to talk to you" he said walking up to them.

"Yeah" Roshni turned to him.

Druv sensed something was wrong he could know from Andrew's way of saying. He tightened his grip in Roshni's hand and came in front of her.

"What is it?" he asked.

"I said I wanted to talk to Roshni not you" Andrew said fiercely.

Roshni saw that the situation was getting heated. She left Druv's hand and held his wrist. She looked into his eyes and assured him everything will be fine and she will handle it. Druv backed off and Roshni said

"Yeah Andrew tell me. Is everything alright?"

"Roshni how can you trust Druv?" Andrew asked. There was silence Roshni could feel Druv glaring at him.

"Andrew what is wrong? Why are you saying like that?" Roshni tried to stay calm.

"Roshni, I love you." He said. Everyone was shocked.

Before Roshni could say anything Druv came in front of Roshni and held Andrew's collar. The whole class had become aware now and everyone rushed to prevent the two of them from fighting.

Meghna felt as if someone just stabbed her. It was the first time Meghna loved someone. She never thought that the entire time Andrew never regarded her as anything more than a friend and used her to get close to Roshni. This was the first time heart ached with pain. She couldn't believe what she just heard and froze there. She felt betrayed and heartbroken at the same time. Natasha kept her hand around Meghna and she was in tears. She walked Meghna out of there.

Roshni was in deep shock she didn't know what to do and what to say. She wondered since when Andrew liked her. She never felt that he had been having feeling all this time. And Meghna? What about Meghna she thought. Meghna liked Andrew. She must be really hurt. When she looked around she couldn't see Meghna. That freaked her out. Natasha wasn't there too. She rushed to the washroom to check if they were there.

Roshni saw Meghna crying on Natasha's shoulders. Natasha had been holding her and caressing her hair. "Sshh.. it's okay it's going to be fine trust me." She said. Roshni didn't know what to say. She couldn't see Meghna crying like that. It hadn't even been a day that she got committed and everything went wrong she thought. Natasha's gaze turned to look at Roshni. She nodded and called her in. Roshni kept her hand on Meghna's shoulder. "Hey I am sorry. I didn't know how come all this happened all of a sudden. Please don't cry" she said.

Meghna was filled with anger when she heard Roshni's voice. She wiped her tears and turned to Roshni.

"You know what all of it happened because of you" she said.

"What?" Roshni said.

"First you told me that Druv wasn't a nice guy. I listened to what you said. I trusted you and now you are in a relationship with him. Were you so jealous of me? You never wanted me to like Druv."

"Meghna.." Roshni's voice choked with tears.

"No you listen" Meghna interrupted. "You told me Druv wasn't a good person. And now Andrew likes you too. Why do you want all guys by your side?" Meghna said.

"Enough!" Natasha shouted.

"Meghna what are you saying?" Natasha asked.

Roshni gestured Natasha to stop "No Natasha she is right. It was my fault." She said.

Roshni couldn't stand there anymore she walked out of the washroom. Natasha followed her. Roshni turned around. "Be with Meghna she needs a friend more right now. I can take care of myself" Roshni said as she wiped her tears.

Natasha knew that Meghna was hurt "Are you sure you will be fine?" she asked.

"Yeah don't worry" Roshni managed to give a fake smile. She stared as she saw Natasha go back to the washroom.

Roshni looked at the mirror infront of her, her face dripping with tears. She knew that Meghna was angry and she said everything impulsively. Maybe she needed a shoulder to cry on but that could probably only be Druv who she didn't want to talk with right now. She didn't know if she was doing anything right. They said that we should follow our hearts and look what messed up shits hearts do. Roshni gathered herself and headed home. She didn't want any more of it and suddenly had a headache.

***

Vishal and some others stopped Druv from fighting. Andrew and Druv were finally taken to two different corners of the class.

"Dude relax" Vishal said.

"He can't just talk to Roshni in that way." Druv said.

Druv calmed after a few minutes and looked around for Roshni. She was nowhere to be seen. He searched some more and thought that she must have been hurt and left for home. He felt frustrated that so much happened and it hadn't even been a day they came together. He wondered how hurt Roshni must have been as so many things happened. He wanted to go to her and talk. Suddenly he spotted Natasha.

"Hey Natasha" he called. She walked to him. "Yeah" she came.

"Are you okay?" she asked.

"Yeah I am alright. Where is Roshni?" he asked. Natasha's face colour changed. Druv didn't know about Meghna's feelings and she didn't know whether she should tell or not

"She has gone home." She ended up saying.

She knew that Druv had sensed that something was wrong. Before he could ask any more questions she excused herself by saying that she needed to head to the computer lab to get some work done.

After talking to Natasha, Druv desperately wanted to talk to Roshni. He felt that something was really wrong otherwise she wouldn't have just left without seeing him. She was bothered by something more than just Andrew's proposal because she wasn't someone who wouldn't check up on him before leaving.

On her way home Roshni wished Druv wasn't hurt. She didn't go back to see him because she knew that looking at him she wouldn't be able to control her tears. She didn't want his problems to increase because of her. She wished Meghna was alright. She knew it must be tough. She wished it was her who got hurt and not Meghna. After all that Meghna had said, all

Roshni could sense was how hurt she was and the last thing she wanted was to see her perfectly happy moments turn into such a nightmare.

CHAPTER 9

HEALER

And the night fell in love with her. Her pearl like tears trickled down her cheeks every night which her pillow soaked. She felt weak for her tears. But the only place where no one complained was at night all alone left with her tears. Her painful tears were wiped by the pillow and the night cried with her without complaining. Pillow became her best friend and the night fell in love with her.

Roshni hugged her pillow and buried her face in it to prevent her voice from going out. Her parents weren't home, still. They had said they will take a little more time because granddad wasn't completely well yet. It was dark and lonely that was the thing she feared the most because she had always been there. But today she wasn't alone. She looked at her phone and it rang.

It was Druv. Her heart felt relief. She wondered if she should receive the call or not. Druv would figure out that she was crying soon and that would make him tensed. But the only person her heart longed to talked to was him. She ended up accepting the call.

"Hello. Roshni are you ok?" Druv asked.

"Hmm.." Roshni sniffed.

"You are crying right?" he said. Roshni didn't reply. "Hey.. trust me I am with you, everything will be fine." He said. She could feel pain in his voice. That hurt her even more.

"I am sorry" she managed to say through her tears.

"Why are you saying sorry? Nothing is your fault." Druv said.

Druv got worried because he could know that Roshni is probably hurt and blaming herself. He knew her parents were not home either. He didn't know what to do. He walked to his garage and took out his bike.

"Roshni where are you right now? Are you home?" he asked.

"I am at home." She said.

"I'll be right there" he said.

"No. you don't have to come it's okay.' She said.

Talking to Druv made her want to cry her heart out.

"Hey I'll be there soon" he said.

"Hang up and go wash your face and please don't cry" he said. "Hmm" She said. "No, first smile." He said. She managed to smile half-heartedly. Even though Druv knew it was not a happy smile. He reassured her that he'll be there soon and hung up.

***

In no time Druv rang the bell. Roshni opened the door.

"You had been in the dark?" he asked and entered the house. He switched on all the lights of her house. "You hate being in the dark and alone so what is this?" he looked at her.

Her eyes were numb. She didn't speak. "Hey.." he kept his palms on her cheeks.

"It is all going to fine trust me." he said.

"How will it be fine?" she asked "How will it be fine Druv?" she said frustrated through her tears.

"Look at me Roshni" he said. Roshni didn't have the strength to look into his eyes. "Look at me" he said moving his palm on her face. As she looked up she felt lost in his eyes. The world around her froze. His eyes were deep like the oceans she thought. Her tears stopped too.

"I will take care of everything you don't have to worry" he said.

She looked away "you don't understand Druv" she said.

"So make me understand shona" He held her shoulders and made her sit on the sofa.

"Meghna likes Andrew." She saw Druv's expression turn shocked she continued.

"I have a friend named Manasvi. Have you heard that name she was in your college?"

"Yeah" he replied. "She had told me that you are just a playboy and you just hurt people's feelings."

"Wait what?" he asked.

"Let me finish. I said that to Meghna earlier. Meghna was getting attracted to you but knowing this made her prevent her feelings from growing. Now Andrew likes me and we both are in a relationship. So she thinks that I did all that on purpose. Maybe I did it maybe it is all my fault. My best friend is hurt because of me." Her voice choked and she coughed.

Druv rushed to the kitchen and got a glass of water for her. He made her drink water and let her head rest on his shoulders.

"I wish it was me who was hurt and not Meghna." She said. He put his finger on her lips

"No why?" asked Druv. "It's okay if I am hurt" she said. "How is it ok Roshni if you are hurt?" he asked.

Roshni didn't reply. Her heart skipped a beat; it was the first time someone made her feel that they care. It was the first time she felt that it wasn't ok if she was hurt. She couldn't control her tears anymore. Tears rolled down her cheeks and she covered her face with her hands.

"You can cry in front of me and show me your face it doesn't look ugly." He smiled half-heartedly but he couldn't make her smile. Seeing Roshni cry made him feel empty and hollow in the inside. He hugged her tightly.

"Hey please don't cry. It hurts" he said. She pulled away and looked into his eyes.

"Please go away from me Druv. I am fire if you come close to me you will get hurt. My life is messed up. Every time things like this keep happening and if you be with me, it will hurt you too" she said.

"I am not leaving you alone. And if you are fire then I am ice." He said. Roshni's heart melted. She didn't know how he knew everything that mattered to her. She was silent. He kept his hand on her cheeks.

"Hey.. I love you" he said. Her tears had stopped "I love you too." She replied.

Druv got up from the sofa and held out his hand.

"Come I'll show you something." He said. Roshni held his hand and followed him to the balcony.

"Look at the sky." Roshni looked up and saw the stars. Druv knew what would make her feel perfect. As she looked at the sky she felt the wind rush through her face. Her heart felt at ease and she felt positivity, the moon was a lovely crescent. She felt Druv's arms around her waist as he hugged her from behind. He pointed at the moon.

"Do you see the moon?" he said.

"hmm" she replied.

"Isn't it beautiful" he said.

"Yeah it tells me something" she said.

"What is it?" he asked.

"It tells me that even though it is crescent right now soon it will become full. It reminds me of how you came and completed me" she said.

"That is so sweet" he said as he felt her silky hair on his face. Roshni felt home with Druv. He told her everything that mattered. Even though things were so wrong in her life she felt happy for some time.

"Druv."

"Hmm" he replied.

"Will Meghna be ok?" she asked.

"Yeah she will be ok don't worry. Nothing was your fault Roshni. Just be with me ok we will get through it." He said. "And I am sorry.

"Sorry why?" she asked "because I got into a fight with Andrew. I didn't like the way he talked to you." He said.

"See now you and Andrew are also not friends. Who is it all because of? I wish I could disappear" she said.

"Never say something like that again" he said and left her waist. Roshni knew that he got pissed. She slipped her hand into his.

"I won't say that again I promise" she said. She looked into his eyes.

"And promise me you won't cry also" he said.

"I promise if I have you beside me I will not cry" she said.

"Even if you do not have beside me, you won't" He said.

"That's not possible you are my life." She said.

He looked into her eyes and pulled her into a tight hug. Roshni closed her eyes and heard his heart beats as they throbbed against his chest. She was happy she knew everything will be fine. Because the one she was meant to be with was now here.

***

"Did you eat something?" he asked.

"No." she said.

"What? Really?" Why do you have to give up eating." He held her hand and pulled her to the dining table.

"Sit here" he pulled out a chair and made her sit.

"I'll make something for you wait" he said. Roshni began to get up from her seat

"No wait I'll make something for us" she said.

"No you sit!" he again made her sit."

"People don't really get to eat what I cook" he winked. She laughed.

"Okay chef Druv. I would be lucky to eat something you cook." He laughed and went inside the kitchen.

After sometime he prepared pasta and allowed Roshni inside the kitchen.

"Here taste a little" he gave her a little in her mouth.

"Hmm... it is yummy" she said.

"Really?" this is the second time I cooked it." He said.

"I can't cook that good even in my dreams" she laughed. Druv stared at her.

"What? Why are you staring like that?" she smiled and asked.

"Keep smiling like that. You look beautiful" he said.

She blushed.

"Ok now sit down let me serve it" he said.

"ok" Roshni sat.

Druv served the pasta and they both had it.

"I learnt making this pasta from my mom. She is really good in cooking."

"Oh, what else do you cook?" she asked.

"Nothing much pasta, pizza and certain other things don't worry you'll get to know as I'll cook them for you." She smiled

"Sure."

"You know since I was a child my mom has always been with me I share everything with her." Roshni can see excitement in Druv's eyes.

"You love your mom and football really a lot I can see that" she said.

"Yeah. My mom was the person who found out that I loved football for the first time and she was the one who gave boost to my dream. Right now if I am playing for the college football club then it is just because my mom supported me" he said.

After dinner Roshni was washing the utensils.

"Where is my jacket" Druv asked.

"It is kept I my room" she replied.

When Druv picked up his jacket he saw a glint of light being reflected from under the bed. He looked under the bed and found Roshni's diary.

"There was no hope only despair. The world had shattered and I was like the walking dead. I fell down, broken and there was nothing but darkness all around me. I ran to find light whenever I saw a glimpse. But I could approach none. Then I saw something.. a hand.. a hope.. and I decided to try one last time.. I smiled and held it trusting you.. and I was pulled out into the light. You became my soul and saw the world through my eyes. You seemed to know everything before I even told you about it. You trusted me and made me realize that I can trust some people in this world. You taught me how pure love is and gave me back my smile which I thought was lost forever. And now, that we are together. I promise to die but never let anything happen to you. I promise to kiss away your pain. I can fight the whole world alone only for you and I promise to not let your smile fade away. Everything bad has to fight me to reach you and I promise I won't let them win."

As Druv read Roshni's diary he smiled.

"Druv" he heard Roshni calling him. He quickly hid the diary in its place and picked up his coat.

"Yeah" he said and walked out of her room and hid in the adjacent room.

Roshni was walking to her room. He pulled Roshni and backed her up against the wall beside the door. He kissed her forehead. "I love you" he said. She looked up and smiled. He felt heart heart pounding against his chest "I love you too. But what happened all of a sudden?" she asked. "Nothing. I just wanted to say this." He smiled.

After half an hour Druv headed home.

"Take care of yourself ok?" he said.

"Yeah you too." she said. He kissed her cheeks

"We'll meet tomorrow in college then" he said.

"Text me when you reach home." She said as he walked down the stairs.

"Yeah will do" his voice echoed.

A few minutes after he left Roshni texted.

Roshni: Thank you for taking care of me you don't know how much that means to me. Text me when you are home. I love you.

Druv: I love you too. I am home.

Druv: Roshni are you asleep?

Druv: Hehe.. Good night my shona. I'll hug you.

As Roshni read the messages with her eyes half open she smiled.

Now that she had Druv by her side she was ok with the world being on the other side also. She was ready to fight for her love.

CHAPTER 10

CHERISH

Roshni: Good morning.

Druv: Good morning.

Roshni: I'll keep my palm on your chest and close my eyes feeling your heart beats. I'll do this every morning and then open my eyes into the sunshine.

Druv: Why?

Roshni: Because till I can feel your beats in my palm every morning I'll open my eyes and the day I don't feel it I'll go into a deep sleep forever.

Druv: That was so sweet shona! Come to college fast if you be so sweet I'll miss you more.

Roshni: Yeah okay then I'll see you in college bye tcr love you.

Druv: Tcr love you too.

Roshni was greeted into the class with Druv's lovely smiling face.

He waited for her at the door and as soon as she came closer to him he held her hand. The entire class stared as he took her to her seat. His face had the expression "everything will be alright

I am with you." She smiled thinking that he had no clue how much strength he gave her.

"So what are your plans for today?" he asked.

"Nothing. My parents will be returning maybe." She said as she settled down in her place.

"Hey actually I had a few doubts in Accounts can you please help me out?" he asked.

"Not now. How about we stay back for an hour after college and I'll teach you?" she asked.

"Yeah that will be good."

"Because I need to complete yesterday's classwork.."

"Roshni you don't have to explain I understand." He smiled and she returned her smile.

Andrew stared at Roshni and Druv as they talked. He liked her but he didn't want her to be sad. Maybe it was just not meant to be he thought. He felt guilty for the way he behaved with Roshni. He had begun to hate Druv who had been a good friend. He realized that he should learn to control his temper. He didn't waned to be with her but he decided to stay away from Roshni because he knew her happiness was being with Druv. He didn't want any conversations because he knew that it would just hurt him. He wished he knew it sooner what those two had, had in mind. Maybe his feelings wouldn't have grown enough to make him behave that way or to be so hurt.

As the third hour was going on Roshni was lost in her own thoughts. Meghna hadn't shown up in college she wished that she was alright. Andrew liked her she thought and wondered how much he must be hurting seeing her with Druv but she couldn't do anything to prevent them both from hurting. The only way Meghna and Andrew's wounds can be healed will be by time she thought. And even though she wanted to be there she could not. Seeing her would hurt Andrew and get Meghna pissed. She didn't realize that the class had been over until the bell rang.

"Hey Shona." Druv came and sat beside her. "Where are you lost haan?" he asked.

Before she could reply she saw Meghna entering the class. She gave a glance to Roshni and went to her seat without making eye contact.

"You want to talk to her?" Druv asked.

"No. she hates me and I don't want to hurt her more." She said.

"She doesn't hate you she was just a little pissed yesterday" he said.

"You know what, you are right I should go talk to her. Even I speak shit when I am pissed." Roshni looked into his eyes after changing her mind.

"Don't worry she is your best friend. Your bond is not that weak. All the best" He said and squeezed her hand assuring her that things will go fine. She squeezed back his hand and got up from her seat.

Roshni sat beside Meghna. When Meghna saw her she was about to speak

"Wait. Let me speak first" Roshni said. "I am really sorry Meghna. I didn't know that I will fall for Druv. And neither I had any clue that Andrew likes me" she said. "I know you are really hurt and if there is anything I can do to make you feel better please tell me" she said.

Meghna couldn't control her tears hearing Roshni's words she started crying.

"Hey.. it is going to be fine." Roshni said as she hugged Meghna. Meghna went on saying sorry.

"I am sorry. I was wrong. Nothing is your fault I was just pissed and hurt" she said.

"Yeah I understand" Roshni sighed with relief. "Gather yourself up Meghna. You are not going to cry for someone who does not love you. I got you." She said.

As she wiped Meghna's tears and handed her, her water bottle. Meghna managed to smile through her tears.

"See that is so good. It suits you. Keep smiling" Roshni said. "Come with me I'll give you a treat today." Roshni said as she got up from the seat.

***

In the heavy bustling of the canteen they made their way to find an empty table.

"Are you done with your homework?" Roshni asked as she kept her the tray of burger on the table.

"Yeah."

"Help me a little with the last question" Roshni said.

"Yeah sure" Meghna replied.

"Where is Natasha by the way?" Roshni asked as she realized that she hadn't seen her since the morning.

"She said she had some work last night" Meghna said.

"I don't know what work" she said.

"I haven't talked to her also" Roshni said. She took out her phone.

"I think I should talk to her" Roshni said as she dialled her number. There was no answer. "I wonder where she is." Roshni said as she sat on the chair.

"Don't worry she must be busy." Meghna said. The bell rang soon and they had to return back to the class.

"Don't worry I got you." Roshni said as Meghna headed to the back seats of the class. Meghna nodded and gave her a smile.

***

"You coming?" Meghna asked Roshni as she was heading home.

"No you go home I have to teach Druv." Roshni said.

Roshni was a little hesitant to mention his name but Meghna seemed to be cool with it. Maybe she was hiding it well or maybe she was actually ok? Only time would tell.

"Yeah ok then I'll call you in the evening see ya." She said as she left the class.

"So we'll stay in the class or shall we go to the library?" said Druv as he sat on the seat next to Roshni.

"I think class will be better because they usually kick us out of the library if I explain stuff. You know they want complete pin drop silence" said Roshni making a puppy face. Seeing her cuteness Druv wondered how beautiful she was.

"So, is everything alright between you and Meghna?" Druv asked.

"Yeah, I am so relieved" she said. But soon her face turned sad.

"What happened?" Druv asked.

"Nothing it's just that you and Andrew were good friends" she said.

"Hey.. it is okay don't get sad" he said. She looked away.

"Ok look at me" he said and held her cheeks with his palms.

"I will talk to him ok?" he said. Roshni's face had an instant smile as she nodded her head.

"Yeah okay. Now let me bring my book so we can start." Druv said and walked to his bag. When he opened his bag he saw the chocolate box that he had brought for Roshni. 'Ferrero rochers' she had said excitedly when he had asked her. She will be so happy he thought seeing those chocolates.

"Druv come on what are you doing?" Roshni called.

"Yeah" he said and zipped his bag. "I'll give it to her later he thought.

Roshni opened the financial accounting book and looked at Druv. "Which chapter?" she asked. He came closer to her and kept his hand on the desk. He looked at the book and said.

"Fifth" he said.

"Oh accounting concepts. Which concepts do you have a doubt in?" she asked.

"Revenue recognition and Going concern."

"Look The revenue recognition principle states that, under the accrual basis of accounting, you should only record revenue when an entity has substantially completed a revenue generation process; thus, you record revenue when it has been earned" she said.

Druv watched her speak and smiled. He wanted her to just keep speaking.

"For example, a snow ploughing service completes the ploughing of a company's parking lot for its standard fee of Rs. 100. It can recognize the revenue immediately upon completion of the ploughing, even if it does not expect payment from the customer for several weeks." Roshni said as she wrote down the example in his notebook.

She looked at him and caught him staring at her.

"Did u understand?" she said.

The window of the class was open and a sudden gush of wind came which made Roshni's hair fly. As her hair touched Druv's face his hand reached out to her face. She couldn't do anything but look into his eyes. Druv tucked her hair behind her ears.

"You look beautiful" he said.

She blushed and looked down. Suddenly the realization struck upon her.

"Hey we are supposed to study." She laughed seeing him embarrassed.

"I don't mind not studying" he winked as he held her hand. She smacked his shoulder

"Study!" she said as she started teaching the going concern concept.

***

"You'll be going by bus today?" Druv asked as they walked on the footpath.

"Yeah" she said.

"I'll drop you." He said and she just replied with a smile.

When Roshni sat behind Druv on his bike she felt protected.

"Be careful we may get into an accident" he had said before she sat.

He never knew that she was ok with it too. She just wanted to walk with him in whatever path he chose. Her grip on Druv's shoulder tightened as he sped the bike. She had never sat behind anyone on a bike before except her cousin bro. She had always wanted to learn how to ride a bike and Druv had told that he will teach her someday soon. She stared at Druv's face from the rear view mirror and saw him staring at her already. She had always wanted to be with someone who cared for her and understands her and she had finally got him.

"Your hair looks beautiful" he said as he saw Roshni's hair flying with the wind. Roshni blushed

"Thank you". She said.

"Here we are" Druv said as he took left to the side of the road.

Roshni got down from the bike and when she stared and started walking away; Druv held her hand and pulled her back. Roshni's heart skipped a beat and her breath got heavier as she saw Druv's face was very close to hers. Her eyes closed and Druv kissed her cheeks. He moved away and allowed her to open her eyes, "Don't worry I am not kissing you" he said as he laughed.

Roshni blushed with embarrassment and smacked his shoulder. "I hate you" she said.

"Really?" Druv raised his eyebrows which made Roshni blush again.

"Hey look here" Druv made her look into his eyes. "Take care of yourself and keep blushing like that you look good." he winked at her.

"You too take care of yourself. Will miss you" she said keeping in mind that it was a holiday for two days. She wondered how just staying two days away from him made her feel like a year has passed.

"I'll miss you too shona but don't worry we'll meet after two days." He smiled and took out the Ferrero Rochers from his bag and gave it to her.

"Omg thank you" Roshni said her eye light up. "You remembered what I liked" she said.

Yes obviously. If I don't, who would? And if you miss me too much then I'll come to meet you"

"No no its okay." She said as she bid a goodbye.

CHAPTER 11

ACCEPTANCE

"Lovely evenings, smiley mornings and dreamy nights once again got their paths turned and joined to mine. Just hoping these lovely days to not end ever and continue living in this wonderful fresh air and breathing deeply the scents of happiness and love which are impossible to smell in the best of flowers or dreams. Kicking away everything that is depressing and tries to even touch me and living my life to the fullest"

As Roshni closed her diary she heard her doorbell ringing. She wondered who it was at that time of the afternoon, unless of course it was her parents who were supposed to be returned right about now. When she opened the door knob she saw her mom's smiling face. She hugged her mom before she could speak

"I missed you so much ma" she said.

"I missed you too my baby" her mom said returning her hug.

"Where is dad?" she asked.

"He is downstairs, getting the luggage. He must be coming now" she said. They both entered the house and left the door ajar for her dad.

Roshni helped her mom and dad in unpacking the things and arranging them.

"How is grandpa now mom?" she asked.

"He is good now finally" her mom gave a sigh of relief.

"You must be really worried na ma?"

"Yeah" she gave a heart-warming smile.

"Thank god grandpa is alright now." Roshni smiled.

Seeing her daughter smile Roshni's mom felt relieved that her daughter was alright all these days. Roshni's dad had brought her favourite chocolates for being a good independent girl. No matter how old she grew for her parents she would always be the little child. Roshni felt happy and relieved that her parents were home. Now that her mom was home firstly she will not have to cook all the time and she felt protective of her parents. Her responsibilities reduced and she felt a little light headed as she could concentrate on her studies better. Not like she didn't have any fun when they were away. Her bond with Druv became so much deeper these past few days. She thought.

***

"Hey, what is my Shona doing?" Roshni smiled on hearing Druv's sweet voice as soon as he received the call. She had always loved it when he addressed her as shona.

"My parents are home" she said.

"Oh thank god they are home now I can worry less about you" he said.

"So what are you doing" Roshni asked.

"I was just talking to my friends" he said.

"Oh are you busy I'll call you back later" Roshni was about to hang up when Druv stopped her and told her how important she was. Roshni never expected much from Druv just the fact that he was with her was enough of strength.

"I am good for nothing" Druv said all of a sudden.

"Why what happened are you ok?" Roshni had been on hold for the past five mins.

"I am sorry I kept you waiting" he said. "I understand you don't have to apologize" she said.

"But why are you so tensed what happened?"

"Nothing just that I forgot that you had been waiting for so long and I was busy talking to my friend" he said.

"Hey.. Sweetheart" Roshni's voice made Druv's heart melt.

"I love you. It is ok I know you didn't do that on purpose I know you love me and I am not pissed or upset because of it; Druv let me tell you one thing. You are my life and I always want to be with you. I understand that you have your own life and you need space sometimes so don't worry so much. Just the fact that you are with me is enough for me. I know you felt bad too that's alright it happens. I will never leave you alone until you want me to" she said.

"You understand me so well." She could feel Druv's smile.

"Roshni, go to the balcony and look at the sky what do you see?" Druv asked. Roshni knew that he was going to say some dialog if she gave an expected answer. So in order to spoil it she said.

"Nothing. The sky is empty."

"Very well spoiled." As Druv said those words Roshni laughed.

"That was fun though." She said and sensed that Druv got tensed up and pissed and told him that she wanted to see his face because it must be looking cute. They talked for about half an hour and Roshni heard her mom calling.

"I'll text you soon my mom is calling it has been a long time we are talking she'll think something is going on."

Roshni wanted to tell her mom about Druv soon. Her mom had always understood her.

***

"Mom I wanted to talk to you about something." Roshni gathered the courage to say it while helping her mom with the kitchen chores.

"Yeah tell me" her mom turned to her.

"There is a guy in my college" she said. On hearing just this much her mom understood that maybe she likes someone and turned her attention towards Roshni. She held Roshni's hand and sat with her at the dining table.

"Tell me." she said.

Roshni thought that it was better to keep her relationship disclosed and just tell her mom that she liked a guy.

"I had told you about Druv right?" she saw her mom nodding and agreeing.

"I like him" she said.

Her mom was silent for some time she didn't know what to say she didn't just want Roshni to get hurt in any way. "Is he a good guy?" she asked. Roshni felt awkward.

"Yeah" she managed to say. Roshni's mom put her hand forward

"Promise me one thing Roshni" she said.

"Yeah, mom?" "Do anything you wish to but don't get hurt ok?" her mom said.

Roshni didn't know what to say she loves Druv and they were together and anyway Druv would never hurt her or she thought that it was a promise she can keep. She kept her hand on her mom's hand "Promise" she smiled. Her mom was apprehensive because she knew how sensitive Roshni was, but seeing her daughter give a happy smile she kept her apprehension to herself and just decided to trust her daughter.

***

Roshni sat on her bed and her face had a smile. It was the first time she told her mom about a guy. Druv would be happy if he got to know that she had told her mom about it a little. Roshni didn't want to hide everything from her parents because she knew that her parents will never want her bad. They are just concerned about her. She knew her mom wouldn't tell her dad neither did she want her dad to know because she was not very certain about his reaction. Somewhere she feared that her parents won't agree and she will have to end things before it even began with Druv. But she shook that thought aside so that she can be happy at the moment.

She opened her facebook profile and saw the first post of Druv. He had changed his profile picture. He had been standing with his mom in the balcony and his arms were on her shoulders. Roshni could feel the love between the two of them and seeing him with his mom made her feel happy and relieved that he is blessed. Before she could think and further Druv's message popped up.

Druv: Hey you there?

Roshni: Yeah I just saw your profile picture. You and your mom look so good I wish god always keeps you both happy and together.

Druv: Aww thank you. That was really sweet of you. But by the way what is my shona doing?

Roshni: Nothing I have good news for you!

Druv: What is it?

Roshni: I told my mom that I like you.

Druv: And..?

Roshni: And she was ok with it. She does not know that we're in a relationship so she is just worried that I may get hurt if you reject me.

Druv: Really? I got worried that you will reject me hehe.

Roshni: No I wouldn't. You had no clue how much I liked you. I tried not to but it just happened.

Druv: Since when do you like me?

Roshni: Actually I started getting attracted towards you since you started staring at me in class.

Druv: Really?

Roshni: Yeah.

Druv: I don't even know when I started falling for you hehe.

Roshni: That's okay finally we are together anyway.

Druv smiled seeing her message. He knew that Roshni had to go through a lot to be with him and she never complained about it. He just wanted to be with her his entire life.

Roshni: Druv I had a question.

Druv: Yeah tell me.

Roshni: why did you choose me out of the so many girls out there? There are many girls in college who like you and want to be with you. I don't look very good also. On the other hand people also think that you made a wrong choice.

Druv: I don't really care what people say about our relationship. I love you and I will always keep loving you. You are emotional and that is a good thing. At least you understand the feelings of others. I love that part of you. You are kind hearted. You are really pretty and you have a beautiful smile. I know your heart is good and you love my heart not my looks which is why I love you immensely. The girls out there just want me for looking cute.

Seeing Druv's message sent happiness through Roshni. It was the first time that she felt special and worth something. She was happy that although Druv wasn't good at expressing he tried to express his love for her just because he loved her so much. The realization again struck upon her that he was the one for her.

Roshni: Thank you. You made my day beautiful you don't know how much it means to me. I love you.

Druv: Mention not. I would love it if I can make a day beautiful for you because by writing your feelings down you make my world lovely every single second.

Roshni: That made my day again. I just can't stop smiling. Hehe

She saw that Druv had suddenly gone offline. His mom must have called probably she thought. While he was away she decided to write down her feelings in their chat room so that somehow Druv feels loved too.

Roshni: Mornings of bright sun shines, nights of twinkling stars, air smelling of love, winds blowing softly against my skin, Birds tweeting me good morning, owl biding me good night, the sight of moon making my eyes shine with love. Everything,

everything beautiful came into my life just because you entered my life. With a whoosh you came and brought happiness into my life which will last till eternity.

Roshni eagerly waited for Druv's reply. She knew he would be very happy to see it.

When Druv saw the message he felt really special he could feel how much Roshni loved him and how he had become her world. He wanted to tell her how much he loved her but his feelings rarely took form of words.

Druv: I miss you more reading this I just want to hug you right now. You see? That's how you make my day. Miss writer. Hehe

Seeing Druv's message made Roshni missed him too and she really wanted to see him. Although the feeling of love was a new thing for her she wanted to endure it and live every moment just looking at him. She really feared losing him she thought. She wanted to capture all of it in her heart.

Roshni: hehe.. I can't help it I love writing and I love seeing you smile so…

Druv: Yeah yeah I know.

Just then it struck Roshni's mind that she had to go and buy grocery.

Roshni; Hey I need to go to buy some grocery. I'll talk to you later.

Druv: Yeah sure. No problem. Take care. Love you.

Roshni: Take care. Love you too. ☺

As Roshni stood in the queue at the grocery shop, she wondered how Druv was and what he must be doing. He was always on her mind even when she was busy. He had got her crazy she thought. But feeling the feeling of love was something she got after a long time and she never wanted to let it go. She loved it.

Roshni returned home and helped her mom cook food. After a long time, she was going to have the food cooked, by her mom. That feeling made her hungrier. She had a long conversation with her parents about everything. By the time she went to sleep she realized it was late and Druv must be asleep. She opened messenger to see five messages waiting for her by Druv where he wished her good night and worried where she was.

Roshni: I am so sorry. I got engrossed talking to my parents so much that I didn't see the time. Good night sweetheart. Love you too.

CHAPTER 12

TOGETHER FOREVER

Roshni's morning started with Druv's lovely voice. He complimented her sleeping voice over call. She smiled.

"So what are your plans for today?" Druv asked as he sat up on his bed.

"Nothing much, just shopping with my parents."

"I wanted to ask you something." "Yeah go ahead" Roshni said.

"Will you go out with me tomorrow?" Druv said.

"Mr. Druv Mehta are you asking me on a date?" she smiled.

"Yeah I guess so." She could understand that he was blushing because of his voice.

"You must be looking so cute blushing" Roshni laughed and blushed. "Yeah sure I will come with you."

"Cool so get ready at five am tomorrow. I'll pick you up" he said.

"What? Isn't that too early for a date?" she laughed. She knew that would piss Druv off and she loved to see him that way because it made her love him even more. "I'll be ready don't worry" she said before hanging up.

***

The next day Roshni smiled and her excitement knew no bounds. She was going to bunk college. She would pick up the studies anyway and she had already informed Natasha and Meghna that she wouldn't be attending college. They were way more excited about her date. "You have to tell us every single thing that happened in detail after you return" Natasha had said when she had talked to her. She had told her mom that she was going out with Druv and her mom had surprisingly been ok with it with an assurance that Roshni would call her up often to ensure that she was safe, wherever she was. Roshni was happy as long as her mom agreed to let her stay with Druv. When Roshni was tying her shoe lace her phone beeped. It was a message from Druv.

"Come down I am waiting" that bought a smile on her face. She quickly locked the door behind her and headed downstairs.

She saw Druv leaning on his car and standing.

"Car?" she said as she approached him.

"We are going for a long drive" he said.

He knew that Roshni loved enduring the nature. Not that she had told him. But he could understand that by whatever she wrote as she associated each of it with nature on the other hand he had also seen her looking at the sunrise with utmost love on their trip to spiti valley.

"What? OMG really?" Roshni squeaked with excitement. She was really happy.

Druv pulled open the car's door for her "hop in" he said. It was the first time Roshni sat beside someone in a car. Actually, it was the first time she was going on an official date. Just because it was Druv everything seemed perfect.

As they drove outside the city, Roshni requested Druv to open the sun roof. She popped out of the sun roof and closed her eyes feeling the wind. Wind was Roshni's best friend. When Druv played the music in full volume and the wind rushed against her face while her hand held Druv's hand she realized that the day may be one of the best days of her life it was just perfect. She insisted on clicking a selfie and clicked about ten of them with him where in some she pulled his cheeks and the others he kissed her cheeks. She wanted to capture all of it and live every moment because she knew that things like that rarely happened.

After an hour or so of travelling they stopped near a roadside Dhaba. The area was rural so there were not many good places nearby to eat which is why they settled for eating soon. Roshni was already hungry though. They ordered the best dishes of the hotel. The food was delicious.

"I love eating in places like this. They have the best food" Roshni said happily.

"I am glad you like it" Druv smiled. After having some food and taking a stroll, they resumed their drive.

***

While going back in car Roshni said "Thank you so much. You made my day." as she looked to him. Druv smiled "anything for you shona."

They threaded their fingers together and looked into each other's eyes. Druv couldn't look long enough because he was driving. Roshni kept staring at him wondering how she got such a beautiful gift from god. "I love you" she said as she tightened her grip on his hand. "I love you too" Druv gave a smile.

"Do you mind if we just rest here for a while?" Druv said pointing to her left.

Roshni saw that there was a small beach. The day couldn't have gotten any better she thought. "Yeah sure why not" she said.

Druv parked the car and soon they were both walking hand in hand without shoes on the beach. "Let's sit here" Roshni said as she pulled Druv's hand and sat down. Druv almost fell on her. And the both laughed. They sat comfortably with their legs stretched infront of them. Druv pulled Roshni closer by keeping his hand around her shoulder.

Roshni talked about how she had once gone to the beach with her family when she was young and that was the first time she had seen the water meet the land. That was the most amusing thing for her at that time. She had built sand castles with her cousin brother and collected sea shells. She had kept telling her mom each time after that day that she wanted to go to the beach and her mom used to get things done by telling her that she'll take her to the beach. Roshni was engaged in talking and smiling when she felt Druv staring at her.

She got conscious and turned to her right. She didn't know that they had gotten way closer. Seeing him look so intensely into her eyes her eyelashes fluttered and she looked down. Druv's hand moved down to her waist and he pulled her closer. Roshni's heart beats grew faster and her eyes shut close and he pulled her into a kiss. A chill rushed down her spine and when his lips touched hers she melted in his arms. The warmth of the kiss took away her breath. Roshni's hand moved up on his chest. Her hand could feel his heart beats. Druv deepened the kiss and her hand clutched his shirt. After a few seconds his lips left hers but her eyes were still closed. Druv hugged her and whispered "I love you". She didn't reply, too breathless to speak and they stayed like that for a few minutes.

When she pulled out of the hug the both looked into each other's eyes and she blushed.

"You are my life" he said.

Roshni's face relaxed and she smiled. "I think we should get going now otherwise we'll be late and your mom will get tensed.

"Yeah you are right." he said and they both stood up and brushed themselves.

As they drove back home Roshni took out her hand from the window and smiled. "woohoo" she screamed as loudly as possible.

Druv laughed "Hey stop. The people out there will get scared" he said.

"There are no people here." She frowned. He laughed and pulled her cheeks

"You look cute like this." Roshni's heart melted and she smiled.

By the time they reached Roshni's house, she was asleep in the car. Druv looked at her peacefully sleeping face. He saw a strand of hair falling covering her eyes. He tucked her hair behind her ear and kept his palm on her cheek. "You look beautiful when you sleep like this. I wish you always stay peaceful like this." he whispered before waking her up.

Roshni was mumbling in her sleep and she did not want to wake up.

"Look your house is here sweetheart you can go and sleep. Your mom is getting tensed shona." Druv said comforting her more with his embrace.

In sometime Roshni finally woke up and smiled. Druv kissed her forehead. "See ya in college tomorrow" he said behind her as she sleepily walked home. She didn't reply anything and just showed her hand biding goodbye.

***

Roshni entered her house and sat on the sofa. She switched on the TV but her mind was preoccupied with his thoughts. She loved him and she never wanted to let him go. She just wanted to be with him she thought. She had heard what Druv had told her when she had been asleep. She didn't hear it on purpose just that she was always alert while sleeping too. She didn't want to sleep anymore she wanted to dream with her eyes open. She could still not believe that things in her life had turned out to be so beautiful in just a matter of few months. She could not stop thinking about the kiss. Every time it popped up on her mind, she blushed. The good thing was when she smiled and blushed her mom wasn't around. Although she allowed her daughter to go out with him, it would be very awkward if she knew what happened.

She dropped a message in Druv's inbox.

Roshni: hey thank you for making my day wonderful. I love you. When you reach home, ping me.

A few hours later Roshni received a call from her best friends. "So how was the date?" Meghna asked. Roshni was waiting for that question. She was waiting to tell her friends how awesome it went and how she had the most beautiful day up until now. She explained everything of how they went on a long drive, had breakfast and went to the beach.

"That must have been amazing. Nitish never did something that romantic for me" Natasha said.

"But I think the best thing is that he does his best and he is a keeper" Roshni said.

"Yeah I love him so much for that" Natasha said.

"How are you now, Meghna?" Roshni asked.

She knew that Meghna had really been hurt after that incident in college and Natasha and she did everything to divert her mind. But Roshni knew it had been real tough for her those days especially when there was awkwardness that took place between her and Andrew's friendship even though he didn't know about her feelings. Meghna wanted to finish off her feelings, confessing anyway wouldn't make the situation any better because she knew who was in his heart.

"I am good don't worry" she said.

Roshni could feel her sadness but she didn't want to bring up that topic again because it would upset her more.

"Hey Meghna, we are always with you" she said.

"Thank you" Meghna said. Feeling the relief in Meghna's voice Roshni felt relieved too.

Their subjects changed from their personal lives to college and homework. They talked for about an hour before hanging up.

Roshni went online to check the replies from Druv. There were no replies and his last seen was also of that morning. She wondered why he didn't come online because he would at least say a goodnight before sleeping. She thought that maybe he was too tired after driving so he must have slept off so she didn't call him up either. She scrolled down the newsfeed and looked at his pictures. Druv had been smiling in the pictures. She wondered how magical his laugh sounded. When he smiled the world seemed to be happy. She went off to sleep after a few last thoughts about him.

CHAPTER 13

A DIARY OF MEMORIES

Roshni tied her hair into a high pony. "You look pretty with a high pony" Druv had told her once by moving his hand on her hair. She smiled looking at the mirror and her heart just awaited to meet him. She had checked her inbox but her message for Druv was still unseen. She wondered where he was and hurried to college. She felt angry at him because he didn't even bother to come online.

When she reached college she saw that Druv's seat was empty. He usually came late so she sat on her seat and waited. Every five minutes her eyes stared at the door but he didn't come.

"Where is Druv?" Natasha asked.

"I don't know. He hasn't even replied to my text" Roshni said.

"I am getting worried now" she said.

"Relax maybe his mom took away his phone or something and there must be a reason why he didn't come." Meghna said keeping her hand on Roshni's shoulder to console her.

They couldn't stay beside her long as the first hour began and the lecturer ordered them to take their seats and not loiter around. Roshni's heart felt apprehensive but she tried to stay strong by keeping the hope that he will come to attend the second hour maybe, then she hoped he may come after break but he didn't show up. By the end of the day, she felt detached and her smile faded away.

She checked for messages from him but she got none. Each time her phone beeped, she excitedly unlocked it just to see the promotional messages by the service provider. At first she didn't call him because she thought his phone may be with his mom. She didn't want him to get in any trouble as his mom didn't know about them too. But her heart couldn't stand staying away from him any longer. She dialled his number but the phone remained unanswered. She tried twice but there were no replies.

"Hey please tell me you are ok" she left another message in his inbox.

She didn't feel hungry and skipped her lunch. Her mom would get worried so she just told that she had gone out after college to have food and she was full.

***

When she came back home, she closed the door of her room and sank on her bed. "Where are you, Druv? I miss you.' She said looking at her face in the mirror. Tears trickled down her cheeks. But she wiped them in one go.

"No Roshni, don't worry he must be fine" she said to herself. She gathered herself up and decided to wait for him.

She scrolled down his profile. '2014 has come to an end and I thank all the people who came into my life. I hope you all always stay with me and support me. Love you all. Thank you to all haters who made me wiser and stronger' his status said. He must have written it during the New Year she thought. She wished she met him earlier. She never wanted to waste even a little time away from him. Seeing his pictures made her miss his smile. She could hear the echo of his magical laughter in her ears. She imagined his face when he blushed and when he got pissed. She could not stop thinking about all the moments she spent with him. Her dreams had turned into reality, at first she didn't believe it but now she had started believing it. She had started feeling that she deserved to be loved and he had made her realize many things. He taught her to love in a way no one else could. She read their chats and could not control her tears anymore. She cried and kept hoping but soon was pulled into a deep sleep by her sadness and tears.

The next morning when she woke up she felt numb. She checked her phone but there were no calls or messages. She turned restless and called him again but his phone was unreachable this time. She went to college just because she hoped to see him. Her eyes searched for him each time it caught someone entering the class. She silently sat and looked out of the window.

"Roshni, where is Druv?" She had been lost before Andrew's voice interrupted her.

"I don't know" she stammered. "What do you mean, you don't know? Are you ok? Where is he?" Roshni sat silently for a while and then explained everything to him.

"Should I help?" Andrew said.

Roshni knew that it must be hurting him to see her that way and she didn't want to hurt him more by asking him to reach Druv, but she had no option. The only thing she could do was ask Andrew to go to Druv's house and see where he was.

"Hey I will find out about him" Andrew said and Roshni didn't realize that she was in tears before he asked her to stop crying and to be strong. Roshni wiped her tears off her face and wondered why staying away from even for a day hurt her and she realized how much she was terrified to lose him. She prayed to god for his well-being and wished to see him soon.

"Here take this" Andrew offered her his handkerchief. "Don't cry. Nothing bad will happen I will go to his house now and find out" he said.

"But you don't need to miss classes for that you can go later" she said. Andrew knew that she said that so that he doesn't have to give up anything for her.

"Nah. I don't want to study I want to go for a ride on my bike. Yoo-hoo!" Andrew said. The way he said it made Roshni laugh.

***

"Did you find out anything?" Roshni asked on call.

"No one is opening the door. I have been standing here since about half an hour. Maybe they have gone out." Andrew said.

"I think I'll wait here a little more" Andrew said. Roshni didn't want to trouble him anymore.

"You don't have to wait we'll find out later now come back. And thank you so much for your help." She said.

"Any time Roshni. And don't worry he must be fine and he'll start attending college soon." He said to make her feel a little better.

"Yeah" She said before hanging up.

The next day Roshni went with Andrew to meet Druv but no one was there in his house. They stood there for about two hours and enquired nearby. The information they got was that they had suddenly shifted elsewhere. Roshni felt detached and heartbroken. Just a day before she had, had a great time with Druv and now it felt as if the entire world had been snatched away from her. Her legs felt weak and she kept her hand on the wall to prevent herself from falling. Andrew held her shoulders and made her look at her.

"He will come back trust me" he said. She shrugged and he removed his hand. She didn't speak anything. She didn't want to trust anyone. Everything that Manasvi told came to her mind. She should never have trusted him. She felt angry for having a heart and giving chance to someone she was always warned about. She opened her messenger but her texts were still unread. She never thought that Druv would do that to her. She had been ditched she felt. But her heart didn't want to accept it. She somewhere felt that he would come back.

"Roshni we should go" her thoughts were interrupted by Andrew's voice. She didn't feel like walking. She was lost in her thoughts.

"Yeah" she stammered and gathered herself up. She sat behind Andrew on his bike and headed home. Bike rides had never felt this lost, she thought.

"Don't worry, I'll try and find out something" Andrew told Roshni before she headed upstairs.

***

Roshni's mom sensed that something was wrong because more often Roshni used to get phased out in her thoughts and didn't smile. She tried to skip meals but her mom made sure she ate a little. "What happened Roshni? You don't look fine" her mom had asked but Roshni quickly changed the topic by dictating a funny incident of college and laughing by burying her emotions deep within. She didn't want her mom to know especially after she had been warned. Her mom understood that she wanted to keep things to herself so she didn't bring out the topic again. She just tried to make Roshni happy.

My heart still awaits for him.. he said he'll never leave me alone.. And there was truth in it... I don't know why I trusted him when no one did and why I still trust that he'll return.. My smile has finally faded away and I just wish for one thing; to have him back. He told me he will stay by my side and my heart says he is somewhere out there struggling and missing me too... Each second seems like an hour. But there is no one I can share it with; except him. But he is not there he is gone.. I just want to hear his voice one last time and tell him that I miss him.. I want him to tell me that it was all a lie so that I can move on.. I want to tell him one last time about how much I love him and how I just want to be someone he is comfortable with maybe I can't be his girlfriend or wife all I wish is for him to have a friend.. Someone who he can trust and I'll wait for him no matter what the world says... they say waiting for him is worthless and he doesn't deserve me.. But my heart says that this time it wasn't a lie.. That this time there was some truth.. And that this time... he'll come back soon to take care of me.. God it is my one wish.. Give me my guy back please'

***

It had been ten days now since Druv left. In order to make herself feel better Roshni made up her mind to wait for him. She had gone to the admissions office and enquired about him but no one in college had heard from him which basically meant he was still the student of the college. Andrew helped her out and enquired about him but he didn't really find out anything which is why Roshni thought that Druv would return and maybe he had some emergency work which is why he went out of station. (At least she wanted to believe it). When she looked at Andrew she wondered that he must have regretted being so harsh on Druv.

Or maybe he is just pretending to be okay but deep down inside is as worried as him because they were still best friends.

Her heart believed that he will return so she decided not to cry and just do things that make her happy. But she failed each time. Everything she touched and saw reminded her of him of all the times they had spent in her house and how they had met each other everything. She remembered the last time she heard his voice when she sleepily walked home without turning back and giving him a glance. She wished that she had turned back and ran to him and hugged him for one last time she missed every single thing about him. She wished he was fine wherever he was and she wished to see him soon. Joining her hands she prayed to god while she lay on her bed. That night she could not sleep properly because of her fear. She woke up again and again with sudden jerks and thought about him until sadness pulled her into sleep.

CHAPTER 14

REGRET WEIGHS TONS

"You know what Nitish is going to take me to my favourite place this Valentines." Natasha said excitedly as she sat facing Roshni and Meghna in one of the last benches. "Really? That is great" Meghna said. The two of them looked at Roshni and saw that she sat expressionless. She had been sitting lost in her own thought and in a completely different world since Druv had suddenly gone. They had tried to make her laugh and talk to her about different things but none of it worked. They had also tried to go out with her to make her feel better but she always disagreed. The bell rang and Roshni silently stood up from the bench and took her seat.

During the lunch break everyone in the class were talking about Druv. It was obvious to talk as no one heard about him. "Druv has left college" Nitin said as he entered the class. He caught the attention of many people especially Roshni, Natasha and Meghna.

Roshni went to him. "Who told you?" she asked.

"He took his TC yesterday from college."

"Do you know why he left college?" Meghna asked.

"No I don't know that much" he said and excused himself to go to his group of friends.

The thing that Roshni feared became reality. He had left college again. First he left Manasvi's college and now he had changed college and no one knew anything about him. She didn't say anything because her thoughts had already taken over her. She silently walked to her bench, feeling abandoned and betrayed.

Natasha and Meghna followed her and Natasha held her shoulder and turned her around. She pulled Roshni into a hug.

"I am here with you. Trust me everything will be fine" she said. Tears rolled down Roshni's eyes and Meghna caressed her hair.

"Don't cry Roshni please" Meghna said.

"I understand" Meghna said. On hearing that from Meghna she realized how much Meghna must have been hurt on knowing that Andrew had no feelings for her but her best friend. She pulled away and wiped her tears.

"I am ok" she said.

"Meghna, I am sorry if I wasn't there then it would be good I just want to disappear. I didn't want you to be hurt. I didn't want Andrew to like me" she said.

"It is not your fault Roshni. Andrew does not deserve me, I deserve someone better" she said smiling.

Roshni knew that she said that to make her feel better and she did feel good. The three of them hugged each other and Roshni finally felt a little better.

Before the lecturer entered the class for the third hour Roshni decided to open messenger. She saw that her messages were read by Druv and he was online. A sudden smile emerged on her face and she squeaked with excitement. She started messaging him.

Roshni: Hey here were you?

Roshni: I missed you.

Roshni: Are you alright?

Her messages were read. She waited for his reply because Druv usually took a little time to read. After waiting for a few seconds there were no signs of 'typing' or any other replies.

Roshni: Why are you not replying? When are you coming back to college?

Still, no replies. Roshni's face became sad and she feared losing him. Her nickname on the personal chat screen changed from 'shona' to nothing. Roshni's name was set to shona by Druv on messenger. She kept on messaging but soon his profile picture was removed and the message that displayed on the screen was 'you are not allowed to reply to this conversation.' She had been blocked by him.

In just a few seconds her happiness had again been crushed. Her tears didn't come out anymore. She could not believe that the person who loved her so much has suddenly blocked her and left her alone. She didn't want to accept it. She found excuses to only think well about him.

Not many days passed since they met and promises were made continuously. Dreams were dreamt of tremendously, reality soon turned out to be a dream and then she wanted to forget it like a nightmare. What confused her was whether it was really a beautiful dream or a nightmare. Should she be happy that maybe for some time it just happen or should she be sad that its gone and it may never return. Sweet summer romances were as temporary maybe and not everyone's summer romances turn into reality.

What stayed in her mind was anger and sadness while her heart still hoped that it wasn't him who did it. Her heart trusted him although her mind did not want to. She knew hopes hurt and rarely are fulfilled but what could she do because she was in love. She did nothing but slept because sleeping helped her time pass easily and at least for some time she didn't think about him because time seemed to be longer when she was awake. She wished if he wasn't to return. Then closing her eyes and never waking up again would be a good thing because her existence didn't make difference to him. Maybe her death would.

It had been a few days now and all the people who knew Druv got to know about the fact that Roshni didn't know where he was and had been suddenly ditched by him. She knew that the scenario in college would not be good. But Roshni was not a person who would run away from a situation. Someday she had to face it so she decided to continue going to college.

Roshni was sitting alone on her chair, waiting for her friends. She saw Nandini enter the class.

"Aww where is your Druv dear?" she said approaching Roshni and some of the girls who were against their relationship giggled and laughed.

Roshni controlled her anger she was the last one who would want to argue with Nandini because she didn't really argue with people who were jealous of her.

"What happened? why don't you speak? Did he even take away your voice?" she said slyly and gave a fake smile.

Roshni couldn't take it anymore and she stood. "What is your problem? Were you so jealous of us?" she asked in a soft and crispy voice.

"You used a toy I had left so why would I be jealous." Nandini said.

Roshni could hear anything about her but not Druv or anyone she loved. Even though he had left her she respected him enough. But before Roshni could say anything Natasha shouted

"Enough!" from behind and came between Nandini and Roshni. She turned back to Roshni and whispered "I got this" Meghna on the other hand held Roshni's hand and took her a little away. Natasha and Nandini went on arguing until the lecturer entered the class.

Natasha and Meghna knew that Roshni was not in a good condition and these kind of fights would only get her more disturbed. Because they wanted to take care of her and keep her at least in a peaceful state of mind.

Roshni on the other hand didn't want her friends to get into fights because of her. She was ok to fight her own battles. She knew that Nandini hated her and she was just waiting for an opportunity to speak something. When she was with Druv she was ok with however Nandini behaved because somewhere she felt protective of him. She knew that he would stand by her and take care of her.

She had heard from people around her that Druv had shifted to Vizag. Apparently, he used to talk to many of the people in her class. She was the person who he did not want to talk to. Nandini and Manasvi had warned her but she trusted him and the thought that he had ditched her made her feel devastated. She had tried everything to contact him. She had made an alternate fake account to talk to him but he always blocked her. She tried calling him but her phone remained unanswered. Once she had also tried to reach him through his mom but the phone was switched off. Doing all of this for him broke her bit by bit but she continued till her heart wanted to give up. She hated to be the girl full of hopes and even though her mind wanted to give up her heart was stubborn till it was finally broken.

***

As Roshni took a stroll in the park she heard Manansvi's voice.

"Hey! How are you?" she said as she hugged her.

"I'm fine" Roshni said.

Manasvi sensed that there was something wrong. It had been a long time since they met because at first she was busy then Roshni kept on giving excuses. She had finally decided to meet her after so long. Manasvi knew that Roshni was in a relationship with Druv. Roshni had talked to Manasvi and then accepted Druv's proposal because she didn't want her to be hurt by anything or think that Roshni didn't trust her. Manasvi was ok with it but had warned her to be careful. She just wished that Druv doesn't hurt Roshni. On the other hand whenever Roshni told about whatever Druv did for her, Manasvi had started believing that finally Druv was in love with Roshni.

"Is it Druv?" Manasvi asked. Roshni looked down and nodded her head.

"What happened tell me everything" she said. Roshni looked up with her eyes full of tears

"He left me." She said before hugging her and crying on her shoulders. She explained everything to Manasvi.

"I am sorry I didn't listen to you please forgive me." She said. "Shh.. It's okay I know it was not your fault" Manasvi said. 'And don't worry I will find out what has to be done. Please stop crying." She said.

Roshni gathered herself up and wiped her tears. "I should not cry for someone who didn't care about me." She said. "Yeah that is like the strong Roshni we know." Manasvi smiled.

"Hey I wanted to ask you something. Tomorrow there is a fest in our college would you like to join me? I don't have anyone coming with me and it will refresh your mood also" Manasvi said.

Roshni thought for a moment. She didn't want to go anywhere. She just felt like staying at home in her room and sleeping. (That's what she did when she was depressed)

"Please come" Manasvi said. But she didn't want to leave Manasvi alone and she was right for some time at least she will have her mind off him.

"Yeah ok I will come" Roshni smiled. They walked and hung out in nearby places a little before Roshni went home.

Roshni talked to Natasha and Meghna about the fest.

"I want to go too" Meghna said.

"Yeah I think I'll ask Manasvi if she is ok with it" Roshni said before hanging up.

Manasvi had only met Natasha and Meghna once but she had enjoyed being with them and her main motive was to do something which made Roshni feel better so she was happy that they would come with the two of them.

Roshni dropped a message in their (Meghna, Natasha and her) group in messenger.

Roshni: Guys be ready we are all going to the fest tomorrow.

Meghna: Manasvi agreed?

Roshni: Yeah and she told that her pass will permit the three of us.

Natasha: cool then. See you guys tomorrow. Gud night.

Roshni: Goodnight.

Meghna: Yeah see ya. Good night.

Roshni kept her phone and smiled. But as the night grew darker she felt doomed. She could not think about anything but all the times she had spent with Druv. Her heart cried as she read their chats and she wished to see him again to talk to him one last time and tell him how much she loved him. She just wanted to stay by him. It took her long to be able to sleep. She slept with one last thought that no matter how much she is hurt from the next day onwards she'll smile and keep everyone happy. She will hide her pain in her smile and be the Roshni who everyone wants to see so that no one is worried about her. She didn't want them to get worried for her problems. On the other hand she felt angry that he cut off all communication with her and didn't even care to inform her about what was up with him. Her thoughts consumed her and her sleeps had become restless.

CHAPTER 15

LOST AND FORGOTTEN

Roshni switched off the alarm and curled up on her bed. "Roshni wake up you have to get ready for the fest" her mom's voice faintly reached her ears. She jerked up and sat on the bed with messy hair and her puffed eyes. It seemed as if she hadn't slept since a year. She looked at the time it was already 9. Manasvi was going to pick her up at 9:30. She jumped off her bed and rushed to get ready. "I will come back soon ma" she said and took the elevator.

When she reached the ground floor, she saw that Manasvi's car was turning towards her house. She wasn't late; she gave a sigh of relief. "Come on in" Manasvi said. A day before they had all planned to go together in Manasvi's car.

Natasha and Meghna had also been wearing dresses because all of them were crazy for dancing and wanted to flaunt their beauty. They anyway felt like homeless people going to college and working hard every day. Getting ready to look beautiful was one of the most amazing things Roshni did when she had to go out with Druv but the fact that she had to do it now, without him was hard in itself. Sometimes pain consumed her enough to just call them up and say a straight no to the world of glamour when she felt like shit on the inside. But she knew she had to do it anyway. She knew that it was for the best that she forgets about him. She knew that she had to push herself to go outside because life cannot end in one person. Reality wasn't as easy as Shakespearian plays.

***

The St. John campus had been in its usual bustle and all the boys and girls were dressed up in their best outfit.

"Come on Natasha. Get out now." Roshni said wishing to not spoil anyone's day by faking her enthusiasm.

"Yeah" she said and quickly combed her hair before getting out of the car.

The campus had been amazingly decorated with colourful banners and stalls. Roshni looked around and what would otherwise seem like a happy and fun environment, started feeling like noise. But that busy environment was definitely enough to silence her screaming heart, she thought.

Seeing so many food stalls, Meghna was the first person to get enticed. She pulled Roshni's arms towards the stalls.

"Meghan first let's see the game stalls and meet people" Roshni said.

"No I want to eat. Life is all about eating" she laughed and ordered two patties.

Meghna was busy munching on the patties and watching Natasha and Manasvi meeting people and getting along with them.

"You need to get done faster so we can go and talk with them too. You little foodie" Roshni said which she knew that Meghna was comfortably ignoring.

***

Some of Manasvi's classmates actually seemed to be nicer than her own college classmates, Roshni thought. They weren't seeming to be people who would hurt someone's feelings like that bitch Nandini can. She didn't even think before speaking. Anyway Roshni had made sure that no topic about Druv became conversation and her friends were considerate enough to not bring it up.

They played games in the stalls and Natasha brought a heart shaped key ring for Nitish. Roshni wished Druv was with her so that she could have brought one for him too. She had always dreamt of doing so many things with Druv of shopping, of having lunch every day, about telling him her dreams and fulfilling them with him. But it was all just a joke for him her logical brain was telling her while her heart argued that it wasn't. The babbling in her head was interrupted by an announcement.

"Hello students!" All of them turned towards the stage which was in the very centre of the lawn. "We will be starting a few dance and singing performances in some time. It will be followed by the DJ. "As soon as she completed the crowd cheered.

"Woah! This is awesome it has been so long since I danced." Roshni said excitedly. She was taken aback by how genuine her enthusiasm suddenly sounded. It seemed like her pain wasn't there for the minute when that sentence left her mouth.

The four friends sat on the chairs with some snacks and watched the performances which were organised. Roshni was mesmerized by the voice of few singers.

***

"Those guys are so cute" Meghna said looking at the dancers. The dancers had been standing in front of the stage after completing their performances and talking in a group. After some time, on seeing a guy alone, Meghna pulled Manasvi and whispered something to her and they both headed in his direction. Roshni gaped at what they both may have been up to and also happy for her friend who was supposed to be crazy for a guy in college, Andrew; who obviously created such a huge ruckus.

After sometime when the performances were over Roshni got to know that Meghna had already fixed a date for herself.

"Look he is the guy" Meghna said looking towards his direction. "He is a dancer and we have many same interests" she said.

"Look someone is blushing" Natasha teased her.

"Shut up!" Meghna said. Roshni smiled.

Roshni's heart had started feeling at ease seeing new hope for her friend. Although Druv was always on her mind she tried to stay distracted and smile. Seeing Meghna blush reminded her of the times she used to be teased by his name and how she always wanted to hide somewhere but at the same time loved to get teased.

She tried calling up Druv but her call was forwarded to his mom's phone. When his mom received the call she said that Druv had gone out for a walk and would be back in some time. Roshni knew that he didn't want to talk to her but her heart wasn't ready to agree to it. She wanted him to clear things out before leaving. Ending a relationship without a goodbye was the most painful thing. She thought. She didn't know what abandonment felt like until it consumed her in this awful desperation. She did everything to reach out to him and he didn't get back to her.

The rest of her friends were talking to some of their classmates. Roshni was not in a mood to talk to anyone so she had sorted to sit alone for some time giving them an excuse that she was going to look around and see the campus. She sat on a bench away from the crowd near what looked like a drama theatre.

After a few mins she got a message. It was from Druv. She couldn't realise what she was reading. She couldn't comprehend how much her anxiety was taking over her until she felt her fingers shake while popping open his message. It could be anything, her mind kept telling her.

'Please don't call me ever. I don't want to talk to you' the message said.

On reading that one message her soul felt hollow. She couldn't even cry. She tried calling him up but he rejected her calls and then it came busy which usually happened when he blocked her. She sat there numb and lost in her own thoughts. She wanted to talk to him one last time and tell him how much she loved him. But she couldn't do anything. She felt helpless and she felt grief like she hadn't felt before and she wanted it all to go away. She didn't want to feel so awful but she was forced to live with the mistake she made of trusting someone so wrong. She slowly gathered herself and made her way to her friends wanting to request them if she could leave the party sooner.

***

When Roshni reached near the stage, she heard a loud bass and the crowd cheered as the DJ started playing. Natasha pulled Roshni and dragged her to dance. She didn't want to tell her friends anything and spoil their day so she decided to remain shut for a few more hours. On the other hand, as everything was now over between her and Druv she didn't want to think even a little about him (it was breaking her inside but she didn't want to admit it).

As they all started dancing Roshni wanted to forget about Druv for once. She knew that it may break her but for once she wanted to forget about all of it and dance till her legs hurt. They all danced their hearts out. After a few minutes it had started raining. "Wow" Roshni said as she looked up at the sky. She felt as if it was the last time she was enjoying the rain and her tears. Which she could no longer control mixed with the drops of water running down her face. It was a good thing she thought because when she wiped her face it seemed that she was wiping off the water. The sky seemed to be crying with her for the wounds he gave. But when Manasvi looked at her she saw her hurt. She pulled her to a corner.

"What happened? Why are you crying?" Roshni didn't say anything just kept her head on her shoulders and started crying. After a few minutes she explained what had happened to Manasvi.

"It's done I know it is over now finally. He told that he didn't want to ever talk to me again." She said through her tears.

"Roshni you said you are a strong girl right? Why are you wasting your tears for someone who doesn't care." Manasvi said. Roshni realized that she was right. She wiped off her tears and stood.

"I won't cry, I can't I am a strong girl. And I have my friends and family beside me who love me so I have to be strong. Meghna and Natasha haven't yet noticed that we are out here. We should go back to the dance floor before they sense something fishy." Roshni pulled Manasvi into the crowd before she could tell anything else. Roshni didn't want anyone else to get worried about her anymore. Still feeling her legs shivering and her soul hurting she danced till she couldn't anymore.

***

After an hour of dancing they all trudged to the food stall, tired. Natasha sat on the chair.

"I can't walk someone please get me some food and water" Meghna said.

"You guys sit down I will go get some water first" Roshni said.

Manasvi insisted on going with her but seeing her condition Roshni didn't agree. She soon returned with a bottle of water.

Roshni sat on the chair beside Meghna silently. She hid her pain well behind her smile. They all sat there for an hour and had some food.

"Guys I think I should leave now I have to take mom to the doctor." Meghna said.

"Why, what happened to aunty? Is she ok?" Natasha asked.

"Yeah, just a little fever." She said as she picked up her purse.

"I'll go by my own. Don't worry" she said as soon as Manasvi was about to speak.

"So now what do we do." Natasha asked.

"I think we should just sit and talk about stuff. I am too tired" Roshni said. Roshni didn't want to head home early. Because going home and sitting in her room will only make her think about him and again make her feel upset. She wanted to stay distracted and being with friends was the best way out.

After talking to her friends about various things, Roshni felt at ease.

"Guys I am tired now." Natasha said.

"Yeah! I think we should head home. My mom may get worried" Roshni said.

Manasvi's brother had come to the college because she was late and he got worried because the driver or Manasvi weren't receiving the calls. When Manasvi checked her cell phone she realized that it was switched off because it got wet. She had been so engrossed dancing that she forgot that her phone wasn't water proof. Roshni and Natasha laughed when she freaked out but also made sure that her brother didn't scold her.

***

After a long time Roshni had a good conversation with her parents.

"How are things going on in college?" her dad asked.

"It is going great!" She lied and explained about all the fun she had in the fest while she had her dinner.

After dinner, she called up Meghna to ask if her mom was alright and they added Natasha to the conference. Natasha had a fight going on with Nitish but Roshni was already too mentally exhausted to be able to console her. She tried her best though.

Roshni sneezed and felt weak. She realized that it was all because of dancing in the rain and then staying in wet clothes till she was home. The day had been very exhausting for her. She had a lot of things going on in her mind related to Druv and she wanted to write it all down because she knew that if it wasn't out of her system she may not be able to sleep the entire night. So the took out her diary and wrote.

I just want to be the person who protects him, who he can share all his feelings with, whose shoulders he can cry on. If today I would have to die for his happiness I would not have any second thoughts about it. I feel like understanding him even now after he rejected me. I want to stand by him as his support. I never wanted anything much from him. But he is gone. Maybe our paths will never meet again. But I am really thankful for what I had with him. Maybe for just once all my dreams had turned into reality. They say patience is the key to everything and I think I'll wait for him. I CAN DO IT! I CAN GET THROUGH IT!

CHAPTER 16

A NEW CHAPTER

2 years later

When I first entered Bangalore I hated this place. Maybe because all the people have the tendency to resist change. Even though I hated this place I felt positivity around me. The weather of this place was amazing. It is pleasant throughout the year. The people of this place are really helpful. My new college and friends make my days amazing. I almost hang out every single day here after classes. Everything here was better than it was before but something seemed missing.

Roshni had shifted to Bangalore and was pursuing Master's degree in one of the best colleges Jalan University. Although she didn't really live in a huge city earlier, she loved the place for its peace and didn't want to leave behind Natasha and Meghna there.

"I'll be home late ma." Roshni said before she precipitated out of the door. She drove out of the parking lot and headed college.

She found college very interesting in the initial days but soon she started wanting to stay alone and away from the crowd. It was her mom's dream to educate her in Bangalore because she wanted her to get the best education. Even though Roshni was strictly against the idea of being there she decided to shift just to make her mom happy. She believed that wherever she was it didn't matter because her hard work will pay.

Veronica waited outside the class. She saw Roshni walking towards her briskly.

"Dude, you are late" she said before hugging her.

Roshni had met her former friend Veronica once in the garden near her house where they were both reading books. And after she joined college they met again and became good friends. They weren't allowed in the class as they were already late so they headed towards the girls staircase.

"Great! We have missed the very first class of the day" Roshni said.

"Yeah and all the credits go to you" Veronica said.

Just then two seniors (guys) were walking down the stairs. As they walked past them Veronica stared at them "they are so cute" she whispered.

"Why aren't the people of our class as good as them" Roshni glanced at them and looked away. Druv was the only guy who had caught her attention. And after he left her, she didn't feel attracted to even the most interesting guys. She had closed the doors of her heart and decided to just study. She had already done badly in the semester during Bachelors which she lost Druv and she didn't want any more distractions. Her studies were her identity and she didn't want to lose it.

Veronica stared at Roshni shocked "Now don't tell me you don't find them cute" she said.

"I am not interested. I have a lot on my plate already" Roshni said. Veronica didn't know anything much about Roshni's past. She only knew that Roshni was once in a relationship. Roshni didn't find it important to tell her about anything too. She wanted to keep things to herself because she didn't like being too much of an open book for matters which would anyway not concern others.

"How about we go for lunch after college?" Roshni asked.

"Actually I am going to meet a friend of mine today. He has recently shifted to Chennai and has come to Bangalore for a few days. It has been a long time I saw him today is the only day he can meet because he will be busy with his friends later on" Veronica said. Roshni was ok with it.

"Why don't you come with me? I'll introduce you to him" she said. Roshni was fine with making new friends and meeting new people, she anyway didn't care about dating or relationships anymore, so more friends would mean more fun. On the other hand her mom wouldn't be home, she thought because of a kitty party with her friends so she didn't want to go home early. She had wanted to stay out late, she was sure of it so she agreed.

They attended the classes from the second hour and had breakfast in the college canteen.

"Veronica, come out!" Roshni was dragging Veronica out of the girl's washroom. They had been standing in front of the mirror since the past half an hour. Veronica had been first combing her hair and then applying makeup. "You are not going to a do a ramp walk right now. Guys don't care as much as you are doing things to please them, at this point." Roshni said. Veronica frowned and continued for a little while before giving in to Roshni's stubborn requests.

"I am really hungry" Roshni said.

Veronica had already alighted down the stairs. "Lets meet my friend then we'll go have something. He may be hungry too" she said turning round.

"Fine" Roshni said wondering what a curse it was to roam around hungrily because her friend just cared about guys.

Veronica had told that she had met this friend of hers while she had been on a trip to Vizag. Hearing Vizag made her only think of one person 'Druv', who seemed to have shifted to Vizag according to people in her class, after abandoning their relationship. It had taken her two long years to be able to start living again for her, as soon as she started feeling some comfort she had to shift to Bangalore and start a new life altogether. The worst part was letting go of Meghna and Natasha and not knowing when they will meet again. She lost touch with them a lot and felt lonely sometimes. She spent most of her time watching Korean dramas and reading novels alone but her heart felt at ease when she met Veronica in college. At least she understood some of the things she said and was trustable more than anyone else was she thought.

"Hello! Where are you?" Roshni's thoughts were interrupted by Veronica's voice.

She had probably called up her friend to find where he was. The fact that it was a 'he' did not interest her one bit and she wondered what his name was. But who cares she thought, as her stomach growled.

"We are standing at the college entrance" Veronica said over call. They both haphazardly walked around staring at each person's face. Roshni wondered how she would make out who that guy is anyway, she was just blankly staring at every guy and wondering if they changed directions and walked their way.

***

Soon they saw a guy walking towards them. Roshni's heart dropped as soon as she saw him. She had never thought in the wildest of her dreams that they would meet his way. She started questioning reality.

"Hey! How are you?" Veronica said as she shook his hand.

Druv stared right at her in shock but he made sure Veronica didn't feel it. On seeing Druv stare at Roshni, Veronica introduced them to each other.

'Hi' Roshni said and looked away.

All the memories they had together came to her mind. All the emotions that were buried inside her since the past two years she could feel all of them at once. Seeing him made her want to go on questioning him about every single thing he did. She wanted

151

to know why he left and what pleasure did he get doing that. She had been shattered and broken but she somewhere still loved him with those broken pieces of her heart. She didn't want to see him. Then suddenly those days came into her mind where she cried every night to sleep thinking about everything they had. And how tough it had been to be able to stand on her own feet again and study like before. 'For him it was all a lie' her mind said. By that time her eyes were filled with tears and anger and hatred gleamed in her eyes. She looked up and saw Druv looking at her. She could feel that he had sensed her anger and sadness.

"Veronica I am really hungry and I also have some work so I think I should leave" Roshni said.

Veronica gave a slight smile and excused herself and Roshni to a corner.

"What happened?" she asked. "Nothing. I just want to leave" she said.

"You should have given a better excuse stupid eating is not an excuse."

"On the other hand, I already told him that we'll be having lunch together because you don't have any work at home" she said.

"What?" Roshni didn't want to tell Veronica anything about Druv and her especially when she got to know that they were good friends. She just wanted to keep things to herself and she already knew that Druv will not be meeting Veronica much and will probably return to Chennai soon. What was he doing in Chennai now anyway? Was he out on an all-India tour with his disgusting little feet abandoning everyone on the way? The thought made Roshni chuckle.

Anyway, it was alright to sit with Druv and have lunch. Maybe she can get some answers out of him about why he was such an ass for the most of his life. She thought that he isn't hiding for the mistakes he did then why should she run away from a totally awkward situation? She had done nothing wrong.

"Fine. Let's go for lunch" Roshni said feeling a deep regretful pit in her stomach, right after she said that.

***

During lunch, it was only Veronica who talked the whole time. Druv replied to whatever she was asking. And he kept staring at Roshni. Roshni on the other hand just sat silently and didn't want to even look at him. She was lost in her own thoughts and had lost her appetite too. Although she had a little because she was the one who made the excuse of being hungry. So apparently Druv had gone to Vizag and now shifted to Chennai for his studies. Veronica could feel the awkward silence between these two people and wondered why they were not speaking much.

"I think I will leave. I need to get home." Roshni stood up. She could see the disapproval in Druv's eyes like she used to back in the days but that just made her assured about the fact that she wanted to leave.

***

While she walked home, she thought about Druv. She had got to know that Druv had been studying in Chennai and doing masters in the Commerce stream. He had been studying in one of the best colleges in Chennai. He is now living away from home in a hostel and completed his UG in Vizag. Veronica had questioned about his personal life but he didn't say anything except that he was single. 'Yeah right maybe he just left the other girlfriend he had also' Roshni thought. A year ago Druv's friend Lokesh had messaged that he was in a relationship with some girl even though Roshni didn't ask for any information, neither did she know Lokesh. It was then that she had blocked them and decided to move on because he never cared. Her heart wasn't ready to listen to her but after what Lokesh told it helped her a little. How strange it was that they meet there in Bangalore. Months after Druv had left college Roshni got many messages from him saying 'hi' 'hello' but she never replied to them. She hated herself for falling for someone who faked all of it and seeing him just made her hate him and herself more. On the other hand, Veronica had sensed the awkwardness between the two of them which is why she continuously went on asking questions from Roshni about what was wrong or if they knew each other since a long time. Roshni's mind had been occupied by a lot of thoughts and she told her that she would explain everything later. What kind of a weird coincidence was it that Druv was Veronica's friend? She wondered if this was a Bollywood romance drama or some kind of shitty plot twist in her life to make it more miserable.

As soon as her mom opened the door Roshni hugged her. She knew her mom's hug would make her feel better. She switched off her cell phone for some time and decided to spend time with her family. But Druv's thoughts didn't leave her mind she had to share it with someone and the only people she could tell were Meghna and Natasha because they were the only ones who knew about all of it.

"Veronica has a new friend and guess who it is?" "Druv" Roshni said after a pause. It seemed as if it had been a century that she had mentioned his name it sounded so strange she thought.

"What?" Meghna said.

"Are you ok?" Natasha asked.

"I wish I could meet you and just hug you" Meghna said.

Roshni explained about everything that had happened. She also told about what Lokesh had told her a year ago because Natasha and Meghna didn't know about it. The two of them made her feel alright by telling her things that mattered and told her that they'll always be with her. Roshni wondered how even though they were miles away they made her feel much better than anyone else could. Even though sometimes Roshni was busy they never left her side. They had lost touch the way it used to be earlier but sometimes when they talked Roshni felt like leaving everything and running back to her friends.

"Okay guys, I think I should just go to sleep now" she said.

"Yeah your voice sounds really tired" Meghna said. They soon bid each other goodnight and went to sleep.

Roshni tossed and turned on her bed and tried every way to sleep but she could not. She sat up on her bed frustrated. "Why the hell did he suddenly show up now I can't even sleep what should I do?" she said to herself. She didn't want the chapter of 'Druv' to open in her life again because it was really painful for her those years. She had given up waiting for him. She had been strong enough to start breathing again but her life again took a turn. This was the last thing she ever expected. It was not some Bollywood movie that anything like that could happen. What was the possibility even of that happening? She thought although she had been really tired that day, she could not sleep the entire night. She tried to write but she even didn't feel like doing that. She didn't feel like doing anything at all. 'Great, he came into my life again and I couldn't sleep' was her last thought at 4am before she slept off.

CHAPTER 17

BLEED AGAIN

The next day Roshni woke up with the constant beeping sounds of her phone notifications. She got irritated and unlocked her phone. Her inbox was flooded with Druv's messages.

Druv: I am sorry for what I did.

Druv: Can you please meet me today?

Druv: I know you are upset and its ok but I just need to talk to you a little please.

Seeing his messages annoyed Roshni. 'What does this guy want?' she thought. One moment he threw her out of his life just like she was no body and now that he saw her suddenly he wants to meet her. She started loathing him. She wondered how low he can go just because he can get any girl. She hated the fact that early in the morning her mood was spoiled because of his messages. No matter how much Druv texted she just blocked him. The entire morning, she had been thinking about him and the fact that he was pushing himself again in her life made her frustrated. She pushed her thoughts aside and boarded a bus for college.

She had her headphones on the entire journey and she felt a little relaxed and by the time she reached college she had forgotten whatever had happened or probably didn't want to think about it and let it ruin her day. The best thing about Bangalore was its weather. Even though the night was hard or the day was hard the cool wind that gushed against her face made her feel like nothing else ever did. That was the only one thing she loved about the place. She thought.

"Will you now tell me what is up with you and Druv?" Veronica rested her head on her palm and turned towards Roshni. Roshni didn't want to hear even his name. After what he had done and what happened that morning that was the last thing she ever wanted to discuss. She was trying hard to forget it.

"Nothing" she said.

"I know there is something very fishy will you tell me or shall I ask him instead?" she said.

Veronica knew that whatever it was it had been bothering Roshni really a lot which is why she had turned completely silent those days. She knew that if Roshni told her she could somehow help her or at least be with her. Roshni knew how much Veronica cared for her and she thought that now that the topic had come up she should clear things out and Druv was gone anyway at least that's what she wanted to think even though she felt deep down inside that it wasn't over and that freaked her out. She explained everything to Veronica from the very start.

There were times where Veronica used the word 'aww' but then at the end she was filled with anger. She had no clue that the person who she thought to be a good friend was such a jerk.

"I had no idea that he was this bad" she said lost in her thoughts.

"It is okay I trusted him too. But as a friend he is really good don't break your friendship with him because of me" Roshni said trying to smile but she failed. Telling everything about him made her start feeling those moments and it seemed as if her wounds again opened up which she had been trying to heal since a long time.

Veronica hugged her. 'I am sorry I forced you to come with us. I didn't know about anything. And its ok, I will do as you say he is still my friend." She said. She knew that if she broke her friendship then Roshni would blame herself.

On the other hand, Roshni was right; Druv was ok as a friend she thought. "It is okay" Roshni smiled. "I am here with you" she said as she pulled away.

"Hey let's not think about all this" Veronica said

"Let's go out after college" she said. "Where?" Roshni asked.

"Just somewhere maybe a spa you'll feel relaxed too" she said. "I don't go to spas" Roshni said.

"Then how about we just go for bowling?" she said.

"Yeah that would be great" Roshni said.

The lectures of the day had been really boring. Veronica had slept during two lectures.

They had sandwich in a shop near the college and were going to later head for bowling in a nearby mall.

"Roshni" on hearing Druv's voice Roshni froze. 'What is he doing here' she thought before turning back. She saw him walking towards her and gesturing her to stop. Roshni didn't want to talk to him. She wondered why he was so much after her. Soon Druv was standing beside them.

"Veronica can you please excuse us for a while?" he pleaded.

"No why?" she said.

Druv went on pleading but Roshni didn't want her to go. Veronica saw that Roshni's eyes pleaded for her to stay but she knew that they had to talk a little.

"It will be fine" she mouthed at Roshni before leaving.

Roshni didn't look into Druv's eyes. "What is it?" she said.

"I want to talk to you." He began "I really didn't want to hurt you I am sorry" he said.

Roshni stood there silently. She was determined to just hear him out and leave. Druv looked here and there.

"Are you done Druv?" Roshni said rudely. "I really need to leave right now I have plans" she said and turned around.

As soon as she started walking away he held her hand "don't go" he said. Feeling the pain in his voice she felt hurt. 'Why did he leave if it bothers him' she thought. She had been hurt for two whole years and it had been the worst days of her life. She had cried to sleep every single day and woke up every morning as if nothing had happened. She had done everything she could and he just used her and threw her away like no guy could. All her wounds were again renewed it seemed. She turned around and removed his hand.

"Don't you dare touch me" she said, her eyes were filled with tears. She left him and walked away.

She wiped her eyes and decided not to cry. She saw Veronica waiting for her near the college entrance. On seeing Roshni, she walked briskly towards her.

"What happened?" she said. Roshni silently just kept walking towards the pavement.

"Roshni what did he say?" she asked restlessly.

"I want to go home. I am sorry, I can't talk right now" she said looking at her.

"But tell me what happened?" Veronica asked. But Roshni ignored. She soon gestured with her hand and a cab stopped. "I'll talk to you later" she said before getting into the cab.

Druv stood there on the street and the people around stared at him as if he was a criminal. He looked down when Roshni walked away, he was ashamed of having lost everything they had because of himself. He decided to leave for Chennai and never come back into her life again.

***

Roshni couldn't control her crying as soon as she reached home. She burst out into tears and clenched her fists in her room in front of the mirror. "Why did you do this to me Druv?" she whispered under her breath. "Why did you come into my life again?" she said as she sank on her bed.

"Roshni, are you ok?" her mom's voice called from outside her room. She couldn't let her mom know. She quickly wiped her tears. "It will be fine" she said to her reflection. She tried to smile but couldn't. "Yes mom I am fine" she said and opened the door.

She was already in great shock because of him and he had held her hand. She didn't understand what he wanted from her. She had never thought that he would return all of a sudden. She could still feel his grip on her hand. Being near him made her heart scared. She had looked into his eyes after two years it gave the same comfort that it gave years ago. She had felt him being hurt as soon as she removed his hand. Why that would hurt him I am just overthinking.

"Roshni what are you doing?" her mom shouted and reduced the flame of the burner. The milk had boiled up.

"Where is your mind?" her mom asked.

"I am so sorry mom." She began apologizing and started cleaning up the mess. Her mom went on asking her questions but she pretended that she was too engrossed in cleaning.

After cleaning the kitchen slab Roshni sat down at the dining table. Her mom had been really tired that day so she had gone to rest. She dialled Veronica's number.

"Hello" Veronica's voice said after a few rings.

"Hey. I am really sorry to walk away like that, please don't get angry."

"It's okay I know you were upset, so relax" she said.

"Now will you please tell me what happened?" Veronica asked. Roshni explained everything to her.

"Are you ok?" she asked.

"Yeah" Roshni said in a low voice.

What else would she have said? Everything around her had suddenly become so confusing that she didn't know what to do. She didn't know about Druv's feelings she didn't even know about her own feelings. Her past had come crashing at her all at once. She was worried that again Druv would show up. She had to tell him to just go away from her life and leave her at peace she was done with being hurt. She didn't want happiness she just wanted peace.

"Can you just give Druv a message from me?" Roshni said.

"Yeah tell me."

"Tell him to please go away from my life and never show his face again" she said.

Tears trickled down her face when she said that. "I think you should do that work. And tomorrow he is leaving for Chennai so I'll be meeting him one last time at Lalbagh Botanical garden at 2pm before he leaves. I hope you don't have any problem if I do. He pleaded a lot" Veronica said.

"No its okay you can meet him and ya I even I think I'll just text him that." Roshni said before hanging up.

Roshni sighed with sadness. Telling Druv to never show his face again would be a tough task she thought. But she was even not willing to get into the trap she was in before. She opened her messenger and unblocked him. He was active.

"Stay away from me! I never want to see your face again...' she typed and then erased it.

She tried two three times and finally tapped on send feeling like something stabbed on her heart. She knew that this may mean that any doors that may have remained open between them may now shut forever. The thought of it made her scared but she knew that it was important.

Roshni: Please stay away from me. You have already hurt me a lot. And I cannot take any more.

She saw that he was soon 'typing' she didn't want to hear anything she thought. She blocked him and a drop of her tear fell on her phone screen.

"No Roshni you will not cry." She said to herself and wiped her tears.

He is gone now. And tomorrow he is also leaving for Chennai, she thought. Somewhere she didn't want to let him go. She felt as if she should have heard him out. But she also knew that she was no way going to put her heart at risk. She didn't want to be around him because her wounds became fresh and it hurt. "And tomorrow he is leaving for Chennai so I'll be meeting him one last time at Lalbagh Botanical garden at 2pm" Veronica's sentence echoed in her ears. She felt like going and seeing him one last time. She forced her mind to push those thoughts away. He is already committed to someone she thought. Even if he is not committed he is no longer the Druv she knew he had left him and she had to go through a lot just because of that. She had fought to be with him and he left her. 'He played with my feelings' she thought. Maybe he had some problem her heart whispered. But if he had a problem then he should have let her know. He should have at least told her before going away. He would never just ditch her and go if he loved her, her mind said. I can never trust him again. Her mind and heart battled till her sadness pulled her into a deep sleep.

CHAPTER 18

DENIAL

"Roshni can you please pass me the butter" her mom said at the breakfast table. Roshni was busy thinking about whether she should just go and meet Druv one last time. Maybe he had something important to say. She wished he was fine.

"Roshni!" her mom called.

"Yeah" she stammered and looked down embarrassment.

"Are you ok?" her mom asked.

"Yeah mom I was just going to ask you. Actually Veronica is going to the park today. So shall I go with her?"

"Why are you asking me this all of a sudden? You usually go to the park to read books right?" her mom asked.

"Because I maybe late today. And I may stay at her house tonight." she said.

"Yeah ok. Just stay in touch" her mom said.

"Yeah."

Being with Veronica would be a good thing she would feel better she thought. And maybe she'll meet Druv. Seeing him, would hurt her she knew but her heart didn't listen she had to see him. So being with Veronica after that will be helpful she thought. She had called up Veronica and talked to her about it. She was ok with it. Roshni was not going to go to the garden with Veronica. She needed a little more time to think.

After two years we met again. Was it fate or just a coincidence? I tried to stay away from him thinking that it was just a coincidence. But why do I feel like seeing him one more time. Does my heart want to go back to the person again? My heart does not have the strength to do that. It doesn't have the strength to trust him again. He came back again into my life like a storm and all my peace is once again lost somewhere. I had waited for him for a year and then my heart took another year to settle down and think that it was all over. But when he came again it all seemed to crash and break. I have lost my path again and my nights and days end in an endless battle between my heart and brain.

Roshni closed her diary. She was completely perplexed. She looked at the clock. The time that day seemed to go slowly too.

As soon as it was 1:30pm Roshni couldn't think more she decided to just go. She put on her black hoody. There was not much traffic that day because it was the weekend. She took less than 20 minutes to reach. She sat on the bench under the Mango tree and felt the grass under her legs after opening her shoes. It was so peaceful at the park and the scent of greenery filled her hollow soul. She leaned back on the bench and looked at the sky. Soon the clouds descended and the bright blaze of the sun made her squint, the weather was very cold though. She heard the chattering of people from a distance and sat straight. She saw Veronica enter the park. She got up from the bench and hid behind the tree.

Roshni: I am in the park. Is Druv with you?

She wished she could talk to Veronica before she met him.

Veronica: No he's not here yet.

Roshni: I am behind the Mango tree on your left.

Roshni lost track of where Veronica was. She felt a pat on her shoulder followed by a sudden loud scream. Roshni jerked back, startled.

"Oh my god you scared the hell out of me Veronica" she said and slapped her shoulder. Veronica laughed. Roshni frowned but she knew that they didn't have much time to continue with the useless chattering.

"I will just stand here and see him. I don't want to meet him or talk to him." Roshni said. Her face grew expressionless and she looked away. Veronica was about to speak when her phone rang.

"It's Druv. I'll talk to you later. Bye" she mouthed to Roshni before stepping out of the shade.

"Yeah tell me…" Veronica said as she walked towards the entrance.

Roshni saw them entering in the garden. Her heart skipped a beat when she saw him smiling. She ignored the feeling and felt sad. Druv had been wearing a black T-shirt and canvas. He looked smart and handsomely older. They sat on a bench approximately two yards away. Druv looked depressed. Roshni tried to make out what they were talking but they weren't audible. She stood there and squinted trying hard to understand but she could not. After some time, she gave up and just settled to look at Druv. It had been so long seeing him talk. She was curious to know what Druv was talking about since so long. 'He never talked to me that much' she thought. 'Anyway how does it matter now' her brain said. They talked for about an hour. Druv suddenly received a call and he sounded freaked out. Roshni could only figure out that he was stressed. He left after a few exchanges with Veronica. Seeing him walk away, Roshni felt dejected. She felt like running after him and asking him questions she wanted to shout and scream. But she didn't have the courage to do that. She didn't want to be hurt like that again.

Veronica stepped into the shade and held out her hand for Roshni.

"Come on girl. Get up." she said. Roshni took her hand and brushed herself.

"Why did he leave so early?" Roshni asked.

"He got a call from his friend that one of them had got into some kind of minor accident so he had to leave." Veronica said.

"Oh shit. Did you offer him help? He is new here." Roshni said.

"Relax. He said he will take care of it. And as of now I don't really know that he will be leaving for Chennai today or not" she said. On hearing that Roshni felt a little relieved but brushed that relief away.

Veronica sat beside Roshni. "I need to tell you something." She said.

"Druv told me not to tell you anything because you have already move on. But I think it is important for you to know."

"What is it?" Roshni asked curiously. She wondered if he was alright. She didn't know whether she moved on or not but she knew that she still cared a little.

"Druv had to leave for Vizag because his parents got divorced." Veronica said.

Roshni sat expressionless on hearing that. "Are you ok?" Veronica asked.

"Yeah" she stammered.

She had never thought that something like that would have happened. He must be so hurt she thought. Immediately Roshni started regretting taking him to be wrong the entire time but soon the thought struck her that he could have informed her if something like that happened. She could have been his support, she would understand even if he wanted to break up because of that. Druv's mom had known nothing about them did she come to know and disapprove it? Lokesh also said that Druv had another girlfriend was he wrong? Even if Druv was not in the right state of mind he could have contacted at least after a month. Did she not come on his mind? Didn't he care about her? Did he think that she wouldn't understand?

She had thousands of questions on her mind which made her sit silently. She wanted to talk to Druv about it. He must be so hurt she thought. She wished she was there in his bad times with him. It was ok even if he made some other girlfriend. It was ok even if it hurt her but the fact that he had to face such big misfortune in his life made Roshni heartbroken. She could have stayed by him at least as a friend. He didn't trust her enough maybe she thought. She hated herself for not being able to love him enough to make him stay and rely on her she had tried everything though. She used to leave thousands of messages for him till about six months and each page of her diary had his mention each night she slept. But he had just left. Having so many things on her mind she was trembling. Tears ran down her cheeks and she rested her head on Veronica's shoulders. She didn't speak anything just cried her heart out.

"I think I should talk to him" Roshni heard herself saying.

"You are very tired today. I'll call him tomorrow and you can talk to him." Veronica said.

Roshni had been mentally tired so she agreed to it.

But later she decided not to call him and leave everything because it was over anyway. They both went to Veronica's house. Veronica's house had a beautiful interior. Her parents had made sure that she was given the best conditions to study. The intricate designs on the walls amused Roshni. She traced those designs with her finger as she walked.

"This looks so beautiful" she said.

"Thank you" Veronica smiled.

"Would you like some coffee?" Veronica asked.

"Cold coffee" she said a she sat down on the couch.

"It's so cold and you want cold coffee. Really?" Veronica tilted her head as she asked.

"Yeah, I need it when I am stressed out." Roshni smiled "and I don't drink hot coffee."

"Okay as you wish." "Do you need help?" Roshni asked.

"No I'll do it you just relax for now." Roshni wanted to help but she felt weak and resorted to listen to Veronica.

Roshni took her diary out from her bag.

It was like a dream come true meeting someone like you. My heart does not accept the fact that you left. Only one question comes to my mind. Was it all a lie? The promises you made. About horse riding and running holding hands. Was it all a lie when you told you'll never let me cry again? Maybe it was maybe it wasn't. I don't know what the world wants for us. And I don't know what you want for us. But if you just come back and hold my hand I promise that we can get through anything in this world. I know you can't stop loving me in a night. And i know about your life. You trust me and I don't want to harm you in any way. Just come back and just once tell me the truth trust me once and don't fear to lose me after the truth... I wish you a lifetime of happiness to wherever you go. Knowing you I got to know that the girl you'll be with will be a lucky one. Take care of yourself. Love you

It had been a year now that she had written it. She wondered how much she loved him and was ready to understand him. She had thought about everything that could be and could even accept him if he came back at that time. Now time had healed a lot of it. She didn't want to get back with him. She had realised that trust is a rare commodity and sometimes love can never be enough. Her love story was like a summer romance which happened for a season and can never happen again. But she knew that she needed a mature love, because not every sweet summer romance turns into how the movie notebook turned out to be. How much the world had told her about romance shaped reality for her back in the days. But the reality is not that simple. She may not want him to die or be hurt but she couldn't live with someone who felt leaving was an option for him when he was all she got.

By the time Veronica returned with coffee, Roshni was cold.

"Can you bring a blanket" Roshni said. Veronica nodded.

"Do you want to watch a movie too?" she asked.

"Yeah."

"Okay" Veronica said.

They watched a movie and Roshni slowly sipped her coffee. Roshni slept off in the couch while watching the movie. Since she was very tired Veronica didn't wake her up or even ask her to go to the bed.

CHAPTER 19

A SIGHT TO BEHOLD

1 week later

"It is so sunny here" Roshni said pulling her hat closer to her face.

"Roshni, wait!" Natasha called out.

Veronica and Natasha were coming behind her with their luggage. Roshni turned behind to see the two of them struggling. She went to help them.

"Oh my god! What did you get in this!" Roshni asked Veronica as she lifted the duffle bag.

Roshni was seeing the Chennai International airport for the first time. In fact, she was in Chennai for the first time. Natasha, Meghna and Roshni had been planning for a trip to Chennai since a long time and finally they were there. Meghna's parents didn't allow her. Natasha had made it though. It had been only a few months she hadn't seen Natasha but when they met it felt like a year had passed. The thought that Druv was in Chennai had disturbed Roshni way too much and she wasn't even willing to go. But knowing that it was the only way she would meet Natasha and feel better she had to agree. They took a cab to Hotel Green Horizon.

Roshni preferred a separate room while Natasha and Veronica shared one. Roshni just wanted some time for herself because of which she opted for it. They had been in the hotel room the entire day gossiping and watching movies. "I feel so relaxed" Natasha said as she pulled the blanket. After a long time they were away from their hectic daily life and some change took place in their lives.

The thing that was on Roshni's mind and that bothered her ever since she met Druv in college was whether she should apologize to Druv or not. Everything between her and Druv was over and she was well aware of that but knowing that she had misunderstood him for a long time made her feel guilty. Maybe Druv hurt her and he left her but she never wanted anything bad for him. Maybe he had another girlfriend but it must have hurt him more than anything to see his parents separate. Divorces were supposed to ruin the mental health of children and maybe that made Druv insecure about what he had with her also. But can that be justified? Can the fact that he abandoned her be justified? Could it be justified that she got to know all this from Veronica and he didn't even bother to explain anything to her? Maybe he was trying to explain everything that day when she just walked away she thought. Veronica told that Druv, his mom and brother lived in a house given as alimony by his father who went back to Dubai. Suddenly all the responsibilities of his father fell on Druv's shoulders. It must have been so difficult for him she thought.

***

The next day three of them went to see the silver cascade water falls. That was one thing that Natasha and Roshni really wanted to see. Veronica had already been to Chennai couple of times because she had spent most of her life in South. Roshni had seen water falls only once in her life in Shillong and she could never forget the beauty of it.

"Wow!" Roshni and Natasha squeaked with excitement.

The water from the cliff rushed down in steps. The pace of water was enough to make mist emerge as soon as the water hit the ground. There was a consistent music of water rushing but it still seemed so peaceful and serene. The wind was cool around there because of the water and it was the most beautiful thing a person could ever see in his life. Roshni closed her eyes and spread her hands beside her to feel the wind touch her. They all stood there for about an hour enduring the beauty of it. That was something Roshni would never get bored of. Nature definitely had its own healing power and its own divinity.

"Let's stay for some more time please" she requested. But Natasha was starving so they had to go for lunch.

"What all do you guys want to order?" Veronica asked. Just then her phone beeped.

Druv: You are in Chennai?

Druv's message popped up on Veronica's lock screen. On seeing that she wondered how he got to know then she realize that it must be her social media profile.

She looked at Roshni. Roshni was busy explaining about her trip to Shillong. Before Veronica could reply to the text, her phone started vibrating. It was Druv.

"Excuse me guys I am sorry I need to take this" she said before leaving her seat.

"Hello" Druv's said.

"You didn't tell me you are in Chennai. We could have met." He said. Veronica wondered if she should tell that Natasha and Roshni were with her too.

"Roshni and Natasha are also there with you right?" Druv said. That left Veronica in shock how did he know that she thought and wondered what all information she gave out on her profile.

"Yeah" she replied.

"I think it is because Roshni was uncomfortable that you didn't tell me. Anyway you guys enjoy."

"Druv listen..." but the she heard the dialler tone.

He had been really hurt to have hung up like that she thought. She didn't know what to do. She knew he still loved Roshni but she also knew that Roshni had been hurt really badly and there was no way that Druv should be ruining the trip.

"Who was it?" Roshni asked as Veronica got back to her seat. Roshni was in a really good mood so Veronica didn't tell anything

"It was just an old friend. She called like after so long so had to talk." She said.

***

"Do you guys want some coffee?" Roshni asked as she shut the hotel room door.

"Yeah" Veronica said as she sat on the bed tired.

Veronica thought that she should tell Roshni about Druv. He would have been really hurt knowing she or Roshni didn't even tell him that they were in Chennai.

"Roshni it was Druv who called" she said.

Roshni turned around in surprise.

"He knows we are in Chennai. He must have seen it through my status update" she said.

Roshni remained silent and continued her work. "Yes then what should I do?" she said.

Roshni didn't want to show that it bothered her. She did want to meet him and get some closure she thought. Otherwise her wounds would always open up around him and she will stay confused. Until she has a conversation with him, she won't ever know what she feels anymore.

"I think you should meet him" she said. "I will stay with Natasha".

Veronica could understand how tough it must have been for her to say that because when Druv left Bangalore then Roshni couldn't even stand seeing him go. But she still pretended that she didn't care.

"If you don't want me to I won't" Veronica said.

"Actually I think even I should meet him and ask for explanation. He had been in a really difficult place and I misunderstood him in all ways. I don't want to be with him but I didn't want him to be hurt either." Roshni said.

She had to just talk to him and make everything clear. She wanted to know everything he had to say and check if she still had something left for him. Avoiding him was just not doing her any good. Not everyone can handle abandonment so well. She had been so secure with her parents but Druv became her safety net. Then he thrashed her world. She wanted answers because she had clearly been struggling with moving on.

Natasha and Veronica looked at her surprised. "Are you sure?"

"Yeah" she said and handed them their coffee.

Veronica had gone out to meet some of her friends while Roshni and Natasha decided to roam in the hotel.

"Veronica knows almost like everybody here." Natasha said.

"Yeah very much in demand" Roshni laughed.

"Where should we go?" Roshni asked.

"I think we should just see the terrace and the pool and see if there is something good around here." Natasha said. They soon came across the swimming pool. It was dark and the pool was magnificently shining because of the beautifully twinkling lights around it.

"Can we please stay here for a bit." Roshni said as she walked towards the wooden lounger. She lay back on it.

"I'll be back" Natasha said. She had got a call from Nitish probably Roshni thought.

"Roshni you were here?". Roshni was awakened by Veronica's voice from a distance. Roshni had been asleep for more than an hour. She rubbed her eyes and saw her walking towards her.

"I had been searching for you everywhere and you are sleeping here. I called you so many times but your phone was unanswered" she said.

"Hey don't worry I am ok. Where is Natasha?" Roshni asked.

"I don't know "she said she will be back in some time.

"Call her" she said.

"I tried calling her. Her phone is unreachable. Where did she say she was going?" Veronica asked.

"I think she got a call from Nitish. I didn't ask her where she was going. Try calling her again" Roshni said. Veronica called Natasha.

"Hello" Natasha said. "Where the hell are you?" Veronica asked.

"I was just talking to Nitish. I am going back to Roshni. She is near the pool" she said in a casual tone.

"Come back fast I am here too I have something for you guys" Veronica didn't say much because she could know from Natasha's tone that she was very happy after talking to Nitish.

***

"Guess what?" Veronica said as they all sat on the lounger. Natasha had been back in a few minutes.

"What is it? Roshni asked.

"I got tickets for the Coldplay concert!" Veronica said excitedly.

"Wow!" Natasha squeaked with excitement. "This is amazing it will be so much fun." Natasha hugged Veronica.

"Actually some of my old friends are going too. So I brought tickets for the three of us too!" she said. Natasha was dancing and jumping with happiness and Roshni laughed seeing her. Roshni was not very interested in concerts but seeing Natasha made her excited too.

"When is the concert?" Roshni asked wondering if Druv was also one of the old friends Veronica was talking about. She just wanted to not know about it even if he was coming she thought.

"Tomorrow night" Veronica said.

"Actually I wanted to ask you something Roshni" Veronica said.

"Yeah go ahead."

"We have one extra ticket so should we call Druv too?" Veronica said. "I mean see you also said you need to talk to him and we can hang out and have some fun too. You can get your closure also and I will meet him too and it will compensate that we hid the fact that we were in Chennai" she said.

Roshni didn't know what to say. It was a good idea but she didn't want to go out and have fun with Druv it would be awkward she thought. But Veronica was right too. Once she talks to him everything would be over and they would go their own ways she thought. She somewhat feared that maybe that would be the last time they met but she pushed those feelings aside.

"Yeah I think that will be fine" she said softly still not sure it was a good idea to have conversations at a concert.

Veronica: Hey are you free tomorrow let's go to the concert. I have got tickets. Natasha, Roshni, you and me. Tell me, you in?

Druv wondered if Roshni would be ok with seeing him. He didn't want to be around her and hurt her always. She wanted him to stay away from her but their destiny didn't work that way he thought. He would be able to see her at least he thought. But he decided that he will stay away from her and not try to talk so that she enjoys.

Druv: Yeah okay.

Veronica: Okay meet us at the entrance of Hotel Green Horizon. We will all go together from here.

***

"How long will you take to get ready Roshni" Natasha said.

"I just started getting ready wait a minute" she said applying the kajal. For the first time Roshni was getting ready and didn't feel the way she felt for Druv. She realised that she didn't want to doll up for him but for herself. She realised that she didn't want to do things for him the way she did earlier. She may have been healing.

Veronica's phone beeped.

Druv: I am here. Where are you guys?

Veronica: We will be there soon.

Druv: Ok.

"Druv is here idiot, let's leave." Veronica said.

Roshni didn't know how she should start her conversation with Druv. She didn't want to do that in front of Natasha and Veronica.

"Guys can you do me a favour?" she asked.

"Yeah tell us." "Can you please send Druv here. I want to talk to him and finish everything off." she said.

"Are you sure?" they asked.

"Yeah" she said. Natasha and Veronica knew that they needed to talk so they left the room soon.

"Come back soon we'll be waiting outside" Natasha said before closing the room door behind her.

Roshni was left alone in the room. She wanted to clear everything out with Druv as soon as she could and she knew that once they were all together they wouldn't even talk. She had no intention to get him back in her life she just wanted to close that chapter. It had been bothering her too much since the past one week. Now that she was in Chennai she had to get it over. She needed to talk about it and to put her heart at ease and for inner peace. She wondered if calling him to a room would a good idea and started regretting it altogether. He may get the wrong idea, she thought. Then again, everything about him was a lie for long, the least she cared about was him having a wrong idea.

Druv was surprised on hearing that Roshni wanted to talk to him. He had never thought that she would talk to him. He knew that Veronica had told Roshni about his family problem and he thought he would be forgiven. He happily walked down the corridor to Room no. 606. He sighed and gathered the courage to knock at the door.

"Come in" said Roshni's voice.

CHAPTER 20

FIT TO BE TIED

On seeing Roshni, Druv was surprised. She was beautifully dressed in a lavender halter neck mini gown and her hair was tied up exactly the way he loved it. He had not even thought that they would meet again. Roshni glanced at him and looked away. Druv's heart felt sad.

"Sorry" Roshni said without looking into his eyes. "I didn't know your parents got divorced."

Druv's smile emerged and he felt as if everything was ok between the two of them. He moved closer to Roshni. As soon as he took a stepped forward Roshni took a step back and glared at him.

"That does not change the fact that you ditched me in the middle of nowhere and walked away without telling me anything. You never loved me. If you did, you wouldn't have played with my feelings that way. "

"What? You think I played with your feelings? You think Manasvi was right, don't you?" he said. Roshni could feel the hurt in his voice. She didn't say anything. Druv understood from her silence that she believed Manasvi.

"Yes! I had been in a relationship with a few girls before I was with you. But I really loved you. And those girls? I never played with their feelings or hurt them. They had left me. There were a few people in college who hated me. They spread those rumours to break my relationships. Nandini believed them too." His voice cracked. "And you Roshni? You were the only one who trusted me. You made me realize that I deserve to be loved and we should not care what people say. And now you don't trust me?"

"Oh please shut up!" Roshni said. "I don't want to hear any more lies. I don't want any explanations. Trust you? Do you really think I can trust you after you suddenly abandoned me? Did you even look back and think once about me. And suddenly after a year you pop up with messages. So I had no option but to block you. I am not a toy you can't just play with my feelings." Roshni's voice increased. Her eyes were filled with tears.

"I had been admitted in the hospital for two days because I had been having problems. I used to have fever regularly because of too much of workout. Football is my life I could not give it up." Druv's eyes turned red with tears. He turned around and rubbed his eyes.

Tears trickled down Roshni's cheeks on hearing that but she kept her heart strong. She wanted the answer to every single question even if it hurts her. Because it had been killing her from inside since the last two years. She hadn't been able to move on from him because of all that. Her heart somewhere waited and hoped for him all the time.

"Are you ok now?" she asked softly. Druv nodded his head.

"You know what Roshni. You never understood me. You never will. I thought I could trust you." He said.

"You were in the hospital for two days and you didn't even take my calls. Leave calls, you didn't even contact me after two days at least you could have told. In such conditions you at least could have sent me one message. Missed call would be enough to make me feel that you needed me." Druv remained silent.

Roshni knew that he was guilty for letting her that way. He had been guilty because he was wrong and he did that.

"Yeah and your facebook profile. You blocked me and went away just like that right?" she said. Druv was silent. "Or was it your girlfriend in Vizag?" she said.

"Girlfriend?" he was shocked. "Yeah Lokesh told me that you had a new girlfriend. And I was just someone you played around with."

On hearing that Druv clenched his fist.

"He is a bastard. I never had any girlfriend after you. It was tough for me. My mom and dad got divorced and mom got to know about you. She had told me to stay away from you and forget you so I had to block you. I had to go away from you." He said.

"You could have talked to me about it Druv. I would have gone away. Why did you just leave me? You have no idea what shit I had to go through. Everyone in our college humiliated me that you ditched me. I cried to sleep every single night after you were gone. I understand your condition and I know it was very tough but you also knew that I would do anything for you then why didn't you share it with me." Roshni paused and wiped her tears. "I didn't believe much in what Lokesh said and I trusted you when no one did. Wasn't it your responsibility to not let me down? Wasn't it your responsibility to tell me before leaving?" she sobbed.

"You know what Roshni. You will never understand me." Druv shook his head. "It's worthless even talking to you."

"I know I sound selfish. I am sorry for what happened. And it hurts me more than it hurt you. I never wanted you to get hurt. Always wanted to protect you. I would do anything to keep you happy. The fact that you didn't feel it's important to tell me that's what hurt me. I can't do anything. It was my fucking heart that never understood anything. It kept on waiting for you. I tried understanding every single thing but you know it hurts the most when someone leaves without a goodbye. I lost everything. You were my entire world. Just one goodbye would have been enough. At least I would know that you cared. At least I would know whether I should hang on to you or let you go. You left me hanging." She paused and wiped her face.

"But you know what you didn't deserve me." She glared at him.

"You know what Roshni. I am happy that I left you. I don't want a girl like you in my life who cannot understand me. I don't know why I met you again. But it is good at least now I can tell you this. I never thought that you would think so low of me. I don't want your trust. You can do whatever you wish to. I can get many better girls." Druv said in anger.

Roshni knew that Druv spoke whatever he felt like when he was angry. But what he told her felt as if someone had just stabbed her. "You can replace me?" Roshni choked on her tears. She ran outside the door because she didn't want to cry in front of someone who couldn't respect her feelings.

On hearing that and seeing Roshni run away. Druv realized how much it must have hurt her. He wanted to go after her. He wanted to comfort her. He wanted to explain but he knew that it would not help. He knew that he had lost the last chance he could have won her. He froze there. He could not move. Why did he say that? He spoke anything he wished to when he got angry. Roshni was the only girl he could love. He hurt her again he thought. He threw his phone on the floor with anger. He had also ruined the last chance he got. He could have made things better. He could have done something. He sank on the bed and lay there all still. Tears rolled down his cheeks. After a few minutes he gathered himself up and barged out of the room. The door slammed behind him. He directly walked towards the parking lot and headed home. He knew his mom had been waiting for him at home and he didn't want her worried.

Veronica and Natasha saw Roshni wiping her eyes and running towards them.

"What happened?" Natasha asked as Roshni hugged her tightly and started crying.

"I hate him" she kept on saying. She was shivering and she could not stand anymore. Natasha made her sit on a chair nearby. It was dark and not much people were around them which was good as it didn't create a scene. Veronica rushed to get water for Roshni but she refused.

"Why does it hurt so much?" Roshni asked as she looked at Natasha. She cried continuously. She refused to drink water and coughed continuously.

"I don't want to live. He says he hates me. I don't deserve him." her voice choked. She cried her heart out. Natasha and Veronica consoled her for some time and finally helped her till her room.

Roshni lay on her bed. She saw Natasha and Veronica sitting beside her. They didn't want to leave her alone and she hated being alone. "Please go to the concert guys. I am fine. I need some space. If I need you guys I will call you trust me." Roshni said.

"Are you sure?" Veronica looked worried. Roshni managed to smile a little.

"Yeah I promise." She said "and guys I have one request. Can we please leave for Bangalore tomorrow? I don't want to stay here any longer." Roshni said.

"Yeah don't worry. I'll take care of the bookings" Natasha smiled. Seeing Natasha smile she realized that because of her their night had been spoiled too.

"I am sorry because of me we could not go to the concert on time. I know how excited you both were for it." She said.

"Hey it's okay we will go through this together Roshni. You are not alone in it. I know you were very excited to go too. But trust me it is you who needs rest we both are totally fine." Natasha said.

Roshni felt really lucky to have understanding and caring friends around her. She tried insisting them on going but they didn't want to leave her all alone. Both of them hugged Roshni Goodnight before leaving the room.

That night both Roshni and Druv didn't sleep. Roshni cried her heart out. The conversation between the two of them and the memories she had everything came to her mind. Her world came crashing down on her and her soul shattered. By the morning her eyes were numb and she had got dark circles. Her smile had faded away from her face.

Early in the morning Natasha and Veronica knocked at Roshni's door with her favourite cold coffee and some chocolates. Roshni couldn't prevent herself from smiling. Seeing her friends care so much for her she felt good. She didn't want to have the chocolates but she loved the cold coffee it always made her relaxed.

"We will be leaving today afternoon. The train is at 1pm" Natasha said.

"Is there any place you want to go to before leaving?" Veronica asked.

Seeing the different places would make Roshni feel better but she refused. She just wanted to rest a little and try to sleep because travelling would get her more tired. Natasha and Veronica watched a movie while Roshni slept for some time.

"Hello" Druv answered the call.

"Hey are you ok?" Veronica asked

"Yeah I am fine how is Roshni?"

"She is asleep right now. Last night had been really tough for her." Veronica said.

"I am really tired, is there something important then please tell me. Need to sleep" Druv said.

"I can understand. I just wanted to inform you that we are leaving today for Bangalore. Roshni does not want to stay here any longer. I hope you understand." She said.

"Yeah ok. Happy journey." He said before hanging up.

Druv sat down on the couch and sighed. He knew that Veronica must have felt how hurt he was by his short replies. He hadn't slept the entire night and after knowing that Roshni was leaving. Sadness took over him. He felt part of him was missing and sadness pulled him into sleep.

***

"Did you check the room?" Roshni asked Veronica. They all checked their belongings one last time before checking out from the hotel.

***

CHAPTER 21

MY SUMMER ROMANCE

Druv could not sleep the entire night just in the fear of losing Roshni. He regretted saying all that. His situation was already too bad and he didn't know what he should do to make it up. He wanted Roshni at least as his friend in his life because living without her was becoming tough day by day. He had tried to forget her and he knew it was his mistake to just let her go that way. He realized what he lost because of his own mistakes and he felt he could get her back. But he also knew that she would never trust him again. The whole time he was thinking about what he should do. He didn't want to let go off her again he wanted to be with her and make things alright. But Roshni didn't even feel like seeing his face he thought.

"Ugh what should I do!" he curled up on his bed frustrated.

He jerked up and sat on his bed, determined. "Mom I am going to Bangalore!" he said and started packing his bag. He had to give it one last try. He couldn't just sit there and do nothing. He decided to talk to her and give it one last try. He didn't know whether she would accept him or not all he knew was he could not give up without trying. Because if he is able to win her again both their hearts would be together and at ease again and their lives would become happier than it ever was.

***

Roshni entered her room. It was all clean and tidy. She opened her book shelf and took in the scent of books. Many people thought she was mad because of that habit of hers. But it made her feel the beauty of them and she felt relaxed. "It had been a tough time. But now it is gone. It is time to move on Roshni" she said to herself as she started unpacking. She felt positive and stronger than she ever was. She decided to close the chapter about Druv and move on. Now that all her doubts were clear and she did not want to be with a guy who didn't understand her value and who was ashamed to have her the entire time. She felt a huge baggage being lifted from her chest like something very important had started happening. Having met Natasha had made her feel even stronger she didn't need anyone if she had such great friends in her life she thought.

The next day Roshni wore the prettiest dress she had. She wanted to dress up like a princess. She wanted to make herself feel better and enjoy the freedom she had from closing the 'Druv' chapter of her life. It was finally time that she moved on. She was a strong girl and she had to come up in life for the happiness of those who loved her.

"You look beautiful" Veronica said as she sat on the chair in front of Roshni.

"Where did you get that dress from?"

"I honestly don't remember" Roshni laughed. "I feel free" she said breathing in the air deeply.

But when she closed her eyes she felt relief and hollow at the same time. She shook the feeling away.

"Hey today I won't be coming with you. I have some work after college." Veronica said.

Roshni needed Veronica the most that day. She had pretended and tried her best to feel good but it wouldn't be possible without her friend around and Veronica was the only one she was comfortable with.

"What work? Is it really important? Can you please stay with me today." Roshni requested softly. She tried hard not to tell her that but she had to because it was becoming tough.

"I am really sorry Roshni but.." Roshni could feel that Veronica wanted to be there too but she thought the work must have been too important otherwise her friends would never say a 'no'.

"No its okay I will go home alone" Roshni managed to smile half-heartedly.

Roshni walked down the stairs of her college entrance. She was busy texting and her entire attention was on her cell phone, when she suddenly heard people around her cheering. As she looked up from her cell phone she saw Druv kneeling in front of her. She was shocked at the audacity of this guy.

Druv had been wearing a blue suit. He looked up at Roshni. Their eyes met. She didn't know what to say.

"I know I have hurt you a lot Roshni. I know those two years must have been very difficult for you" he began. Roshni was boiling with emotions. She couldn't move or speak anything only stare at him. "I am really sorry for hurting you and I promise I will never do that again. Please forgive me for what I did. I don't know whether you still love me or not. All I know is you were mine and I lost a diamond because of my stupid mistake. I regret letting go off you and it hurts me when you are hurt. You were always the person I loved but when I left, I never thought our paths would meet again this way." He paused a little to control his tears from falling. By this time Roshni had tears trickling down her cheeks. "It had been really tough for me I wish you were there. I was wrong to have hurt you." He had a bunch of hundred roses in his hand. He opened his arms wide. "I love you Roshni" he said loud enough that the college students heard. There had been silence all around them people were watching and smiling.

"Will you please forgive me? Can we please start everything afresh? Can you please give me just one more chance?" Druv said.

Hearing all of that from Druv made Roshni feel angry. He was now waiting for an answer. He knew that the only way he could propose to Roshni and win her again was by publicly accepting her.

He had made her feel valueless and unworthy in the last conversation they had. Although he said that because he was angry, he knew how much it must have hurt her. She was never wrong on her part. He thought, she didn't accept it but her heart waited for him all that time and she had not even looked at any other guy. She was not committed yet loyal. She deserved to get all the happiness in the world. Just proposing to her was the least he could do.

He was the guy who had left her two years ago Roshni thought. He had hurt her and never looked back until destiny made them meet again. He had hurt her and she didn't want to be hurt again. She could hear the crowd saying 'say yes' but none of them knew how hurt she was. She felt weak but the only thing she did was she turned back and ran. She wanted to forget what happened. She wanted to forget that Druv just proposed to her. She had been trying to be strong. She ran like she never did before.

'Roshni wait please!" she heard Druv's footsteps behind her.

"Please stop" he begged.

But then he had no option he ran faster and caught her hand. He turned her around. Her face was wet with tears.

"What do you want?" she shouted.

"I know you love me. Please don't leave me. Please don't do what I did to you. It's hurting me I love you" he said.

"I have been hurt" her voice choked. She couldn't speak anymore. Druv pulled her into a hug. He moved his hand around her waist and held her tightly. Roshni resisted for a while but she couldn't do it anymore after a few seconds. She had loved Druv since so long. It had killed her to not be able to be with him. "I love you" he said.

Roshni pulled away and realised that she was going to finally give the speech that her mind had been preparing since years for her well- being.

"Now, I will speak and you listen Druv Mehta" she said and the strength in her voice came back better than she could imagine.

Druv stayed quiet. He looked hurt.

"I was a perfectly happy person until you came into my life. I never thought I would fall in love with you but I did because obviously I was a human being too and love never comes with warnings. I was younger and immature that time and I believed that if I put my trust in you then you would never break it. That is how I saw my parents. I get the point that you saw something completely opposite to what I saw at home but that can never justify the fact that you were completely ok with leaving me behind. If today our paths wouldn't have crossed then probably you wouldn't have cared to talk to me. Do you remember how you texted me that I should stay away from you? Well, I really think you should be the one staying away from Me." she said.

Before Druv could speak she gestured him to stop and continued, "I don't care what you went through and how tough your life has been. If you felt even for a second that you could walk away from me without even an explanation, I am pretty sure that it was the easiest thing for you to do. And guess what?" she laughed slyly and continued.

"You blamed me for never understanding you. Do you expect me to understand the feelings of someone who abandoned me? Like seriously? The fact that you wanted to manipulate me into blaming myself for something that was completely your fault showed what kind of a person you are. These huge big gestures with 100 roses look good in Bollywood movies where most women have no voice of their own and undergo Stockholm syndrome. This is no Bollywood movie where I will be with someone who can so comfortably abuse Me." she said.

Roshni could see a few people staring at them as her voice grew louder and she sensed embarrassment on Druv's face. "What I had with you was the most amazing thing I felt in my life but you ruined that. You didn't just ruin my love for you when you walked away. You taught me how to live without you every single day without falling, you tarnished every single beautiful thing about my dreams because I associated those dreams with you and you made me never want to fall in love again because I stopped looking at men as good humans altogether. I didn't give a chance to anyone who found me attractive." She paused. "Now don't think like the self-obsessed jerk you are that I saved myself for you." She chuckled and continued "I don't care how many people are listening to this but feelings are not to be played with. You, Druv will always be the wound in my heart that turned into a scar. You can never hold a place more important than that. I will never make the same mistake of being with you so that you can make me walk through the hell hole again."

Druv was in tears realising that the chapter he closed in his life by his own choice wasn't gonna open again on his choice. He realised that relationships were never supposed to work on one side.

"You have to live with the choice you made Druv, and your choice was never me." Roshni completed.

"Now, you have caused me enough pain and embarrassment to stay here" she said and gestured towards the doorway. She watched Druv walk away slowly.

"Oh my god" she said to herself as she supported her knees to sit down on the couch near the reception. She had never wanted so much to shout at someone. It was the first time she felt strong to stand up to someone who had hurt her for so long. She felt slightly guilty as it was a little out of her character to come out so strong and firm but she felt relieved. She saw Veronica jog towards her "Roshni are you ok?" she said.

"No Veronica, I am not and can we please talk later. I want to be alone right now. I am not in the headspace to talk." She said.

"Okay. Call me up if you need anything." Veronica left after giving her friend a side hug.

It was in that moment that Roshni felt like someone she had been wanting back in her life, wasn't worth it. She realised that she needed to respect herself first before she chooses someone for herself. She couldn't go back to someone who never saw how valuable she was. She had known about herself that she loved with all her heart and that she would never do to someone what Druv did to her. There were lots of broken people everywhere but someone's brokenness cannot be a justified enough reason for them to hurt and break others. She never regretted the love she gave to Druv, maybe he needed it. She would always cherish her Summer Romance with him and probably no one in her life would make her feel like that again. But she needed Druv's apology to heal and she needed to tell herself that he is no longer the reason for her happiness.

She looked at the staircase and saw a cute guy staring at her. She smiled and sighed with relief. Her heart has healed now and she was ready for a new journey.

Epilogue

We all seek out love because it is an essential and rare commodity. We often ask the question about what money can't buy and the answer is always something we feel internally. There are different love languages in which we express the magnificence of our feelings but sometimes we need to wake up and realise that life isn't a dream, and some stories are meant to not happen because better things are coming our way.

Sometimes the world around us wants us to believe the lies so that living becomes easier but no one told that the truth may look hard, but is always the thing that makes life easier. Some conversations are hard to have, some moves are hard to make and sometimes we make mistakes but what matters is that we need to save ourselves.

Fairy tales help us heart become happy with lies because we need hope to survive. There is sometimes never a prince charming coming to save us, by the time we start growing up we start realising that we are the heroes of our lives, we have to be since we have no choice.

The choices we make shapes what happens to us and with us and that's why we need to choose wisely.

Summer Romances happens in people's lives and after a season everything ends but the devastating consequences of a heartbreak or a painful breakup is not something someone wants to talk about.

Sometimes we need to experience these summer romances to make us choose wiser and make better choices.

Choices at the same time may not be life sentences since we can change them anytime we want and we are just one choice away from completely different life.

To all the folks who have experienced heartbreaks – I am proud of you for having the courage to open your heart up again to the world after realising how harsh it can get sometimes.

XOXO

ANUSHKA AGRAWAL

Author of *Bad Bitch Philosophy: A self-worth guide.*

www.ingramcontent.com/pod-product-compliance
Lightning Source LLC
LaVergne TN
LVHW041514170726
843492LV00005B/1495